FIRST FORCE PUSH

CARA DUNE

SNACK TIME

IG-11

THE MANDALORIAN

JAWAS

IG-11

LEGENDARY WARRIOR
GREATEST IN THE GALAXY

ARMORER

BOUNTY HUNTER

FIRST TRIP OUT

UGNAUGHT

GROGU

STAR WARS
THE
MANDALORIAN

THE MANDALORIAN

The Mandalorian tracks his bounty.

DRAW THE OTHER SIDE OF THE MANDALORIAN'S HELMET.

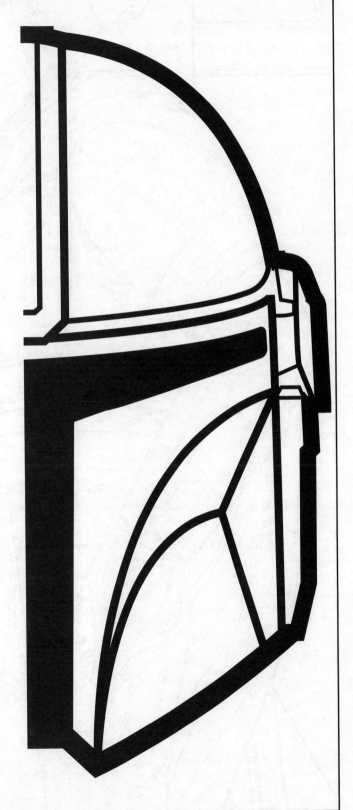

MATCH THE MANDALORIAN TO HIS CORRECT SHADOW.

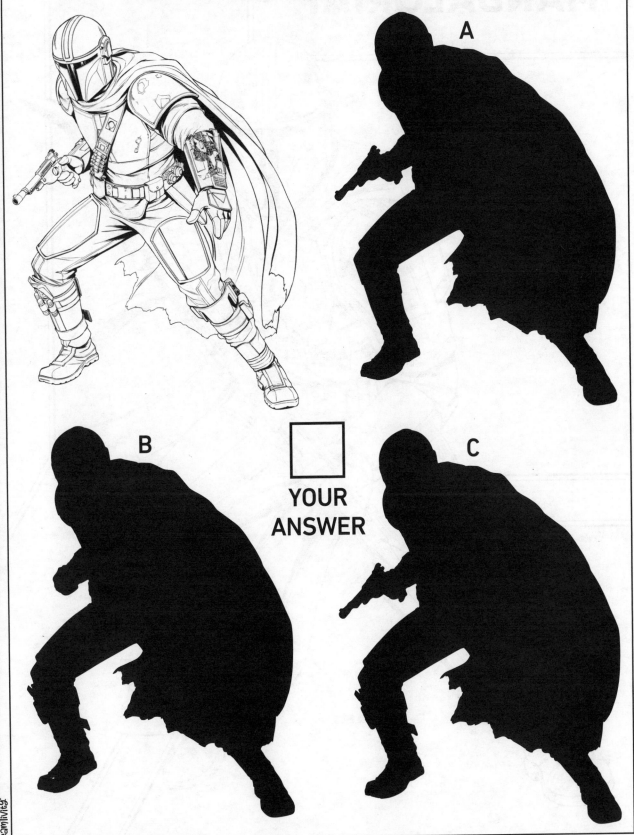

A

B

YOUR
ANSWER

C

Answer: C

THE MANDALORIAN

GREEF KARGA

HOW MANY WORDS CAN YOU MAKE USING THE LETTERS IN:

MANDALORIAN BOUNTY HUNTER

_____   _____

_____   _____

_____   _____

                                _____

                                _____

                                _____

                                _____

                                _____

The Mandalorian prepares to accept his next assignment.

KUIIL & BLURRG

THE MANDALORIAN

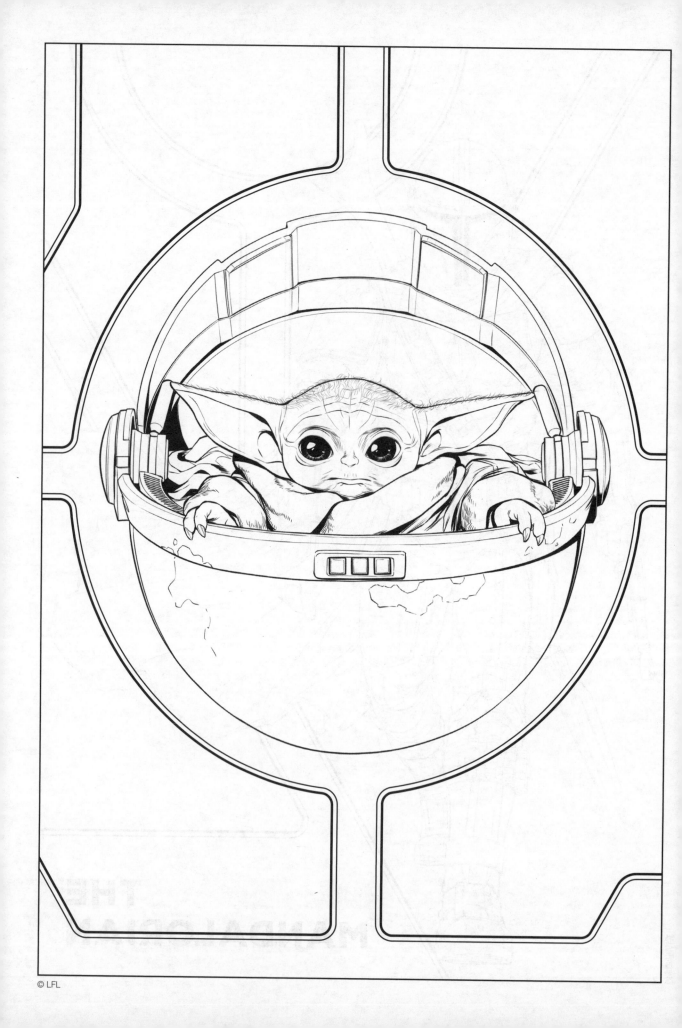

GROGU

DOTS AND BOXES

Take turns connecting two dots next to each other. The player who draws the final line to complete a box wins that box and writes his initial inside. The player is given another turn. Play until all dots are connected.

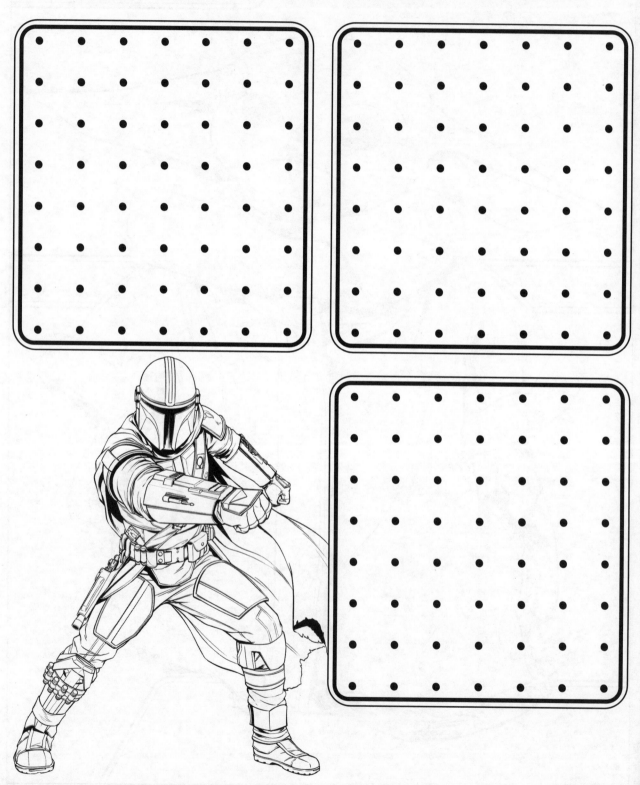

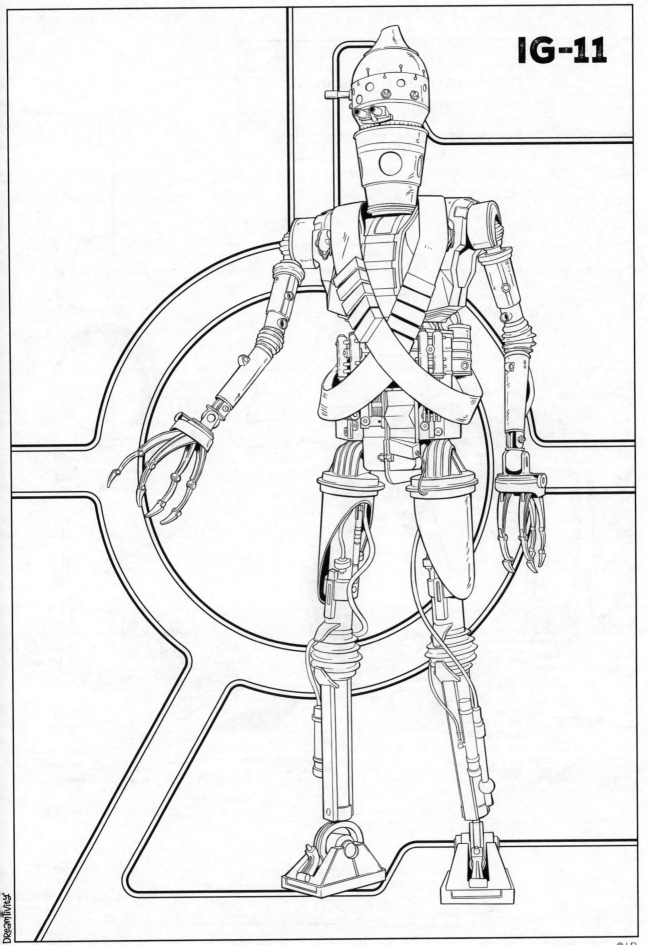

IG-11

The Mandalorian arrives and is ready for action.

CARA
DUNE

**THE
ARMORER**

WHICH LINE LEADS THE MANDALORIAN TO GROGU?

A   B   C

YOUR
ANSWER

Answer: A

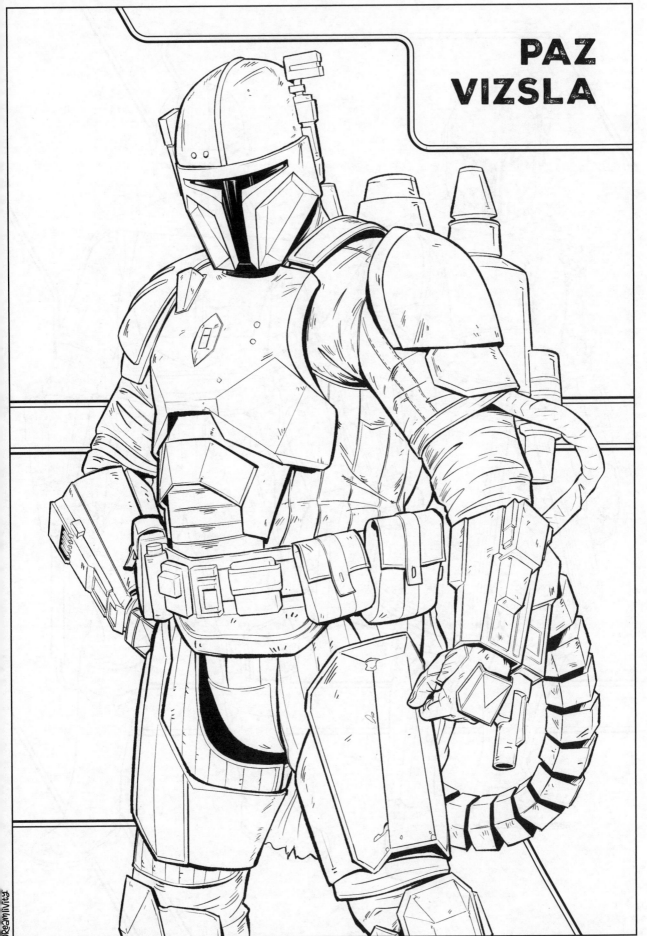

PAZ VIZSLA

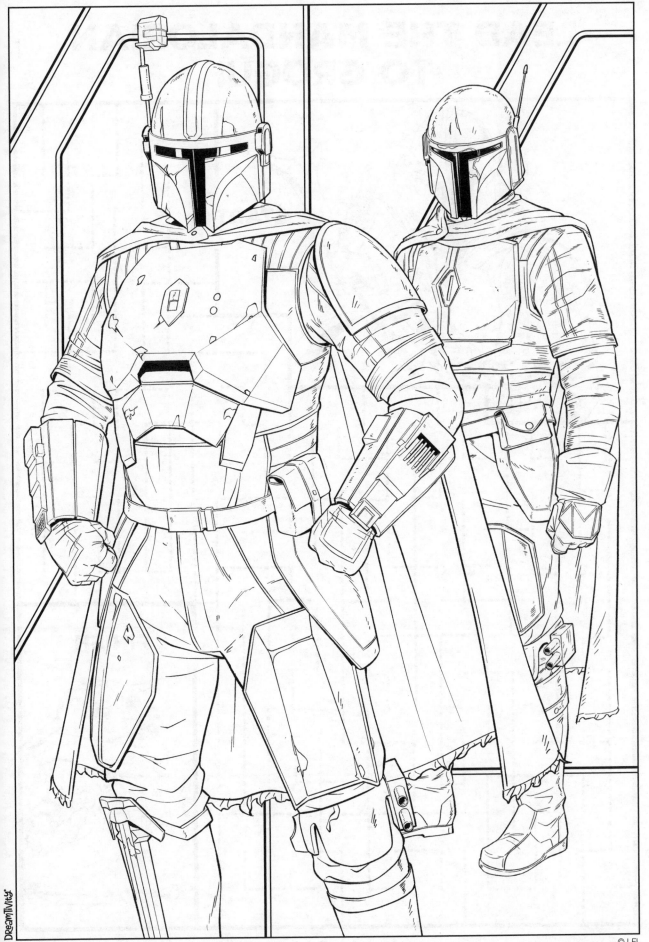

LEAD THE MANDALORIAN TO GROGU.

START

FINISH

© LFL

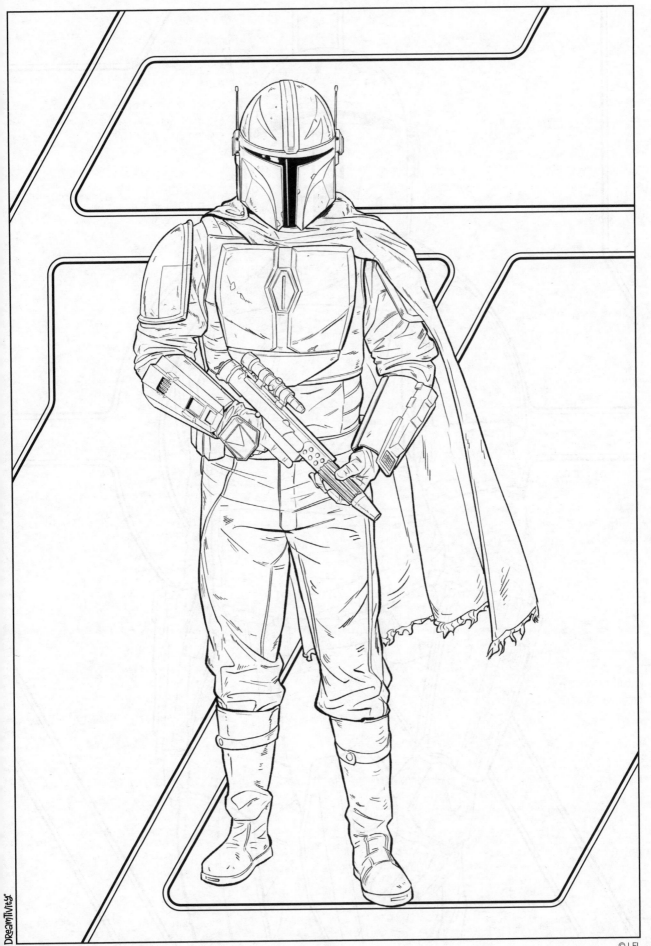

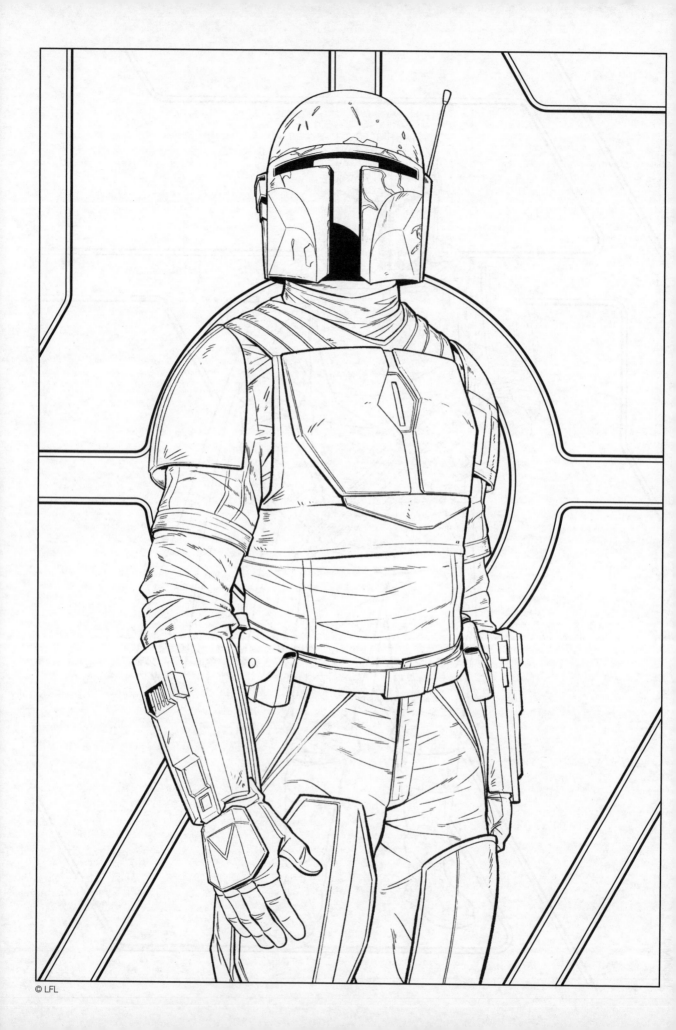

© LFL

WHICH ARMORER
IS DIFFERENT?

A

B

C

D

YOUR ANSWER

Answer: C

The Armorer prepares new armor for the Mandalorian.

© LFL

AT-ST
RAIDER

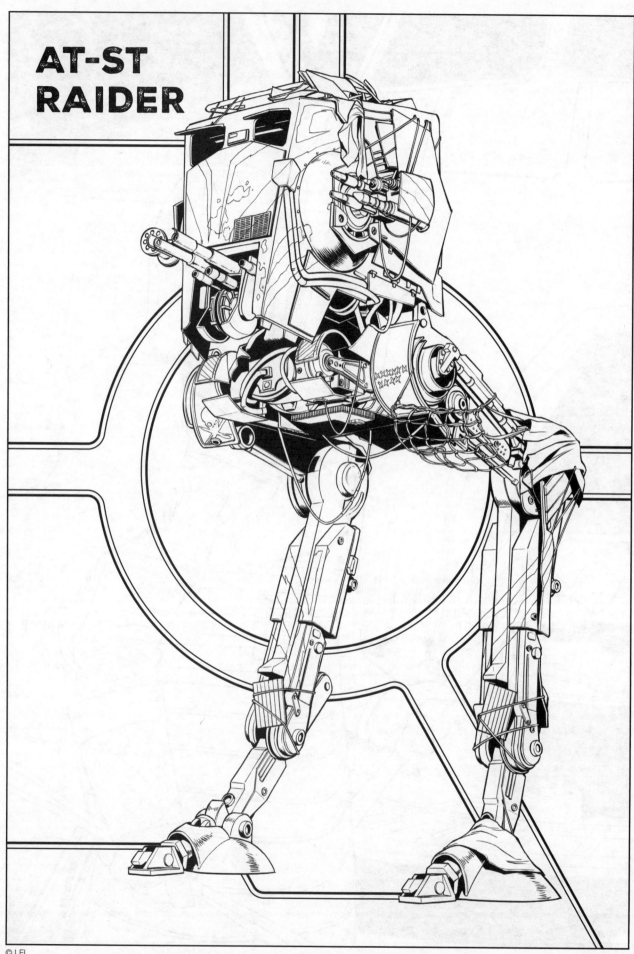

KLATOOINIAN RAIDERS

DReamWRKs

XI'AN

© LFL

BURG

Racing across the desert in pursuit of the next bounty.

WHICH PIECE COMPLETES THE PICTURE?

YOUR ANSWER

Answer: C

GROGU

© LFL

THE
MANDALORIAN

INCINERATOR TROOPER

USE THE GRID TO DRAW THE MANDALORIAN.

GROGU

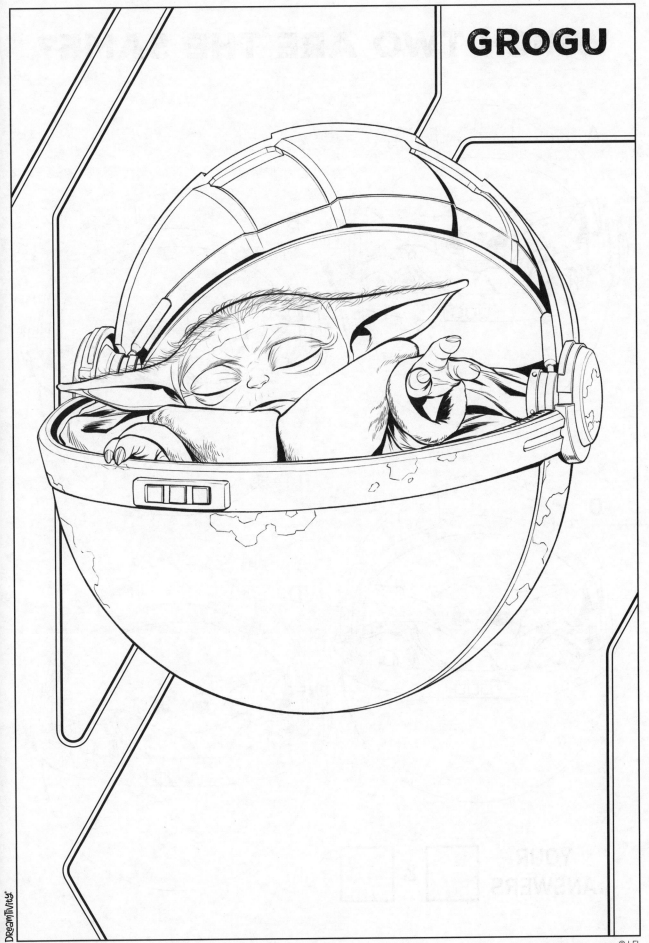

WHICH TWO ARE THE SAME?

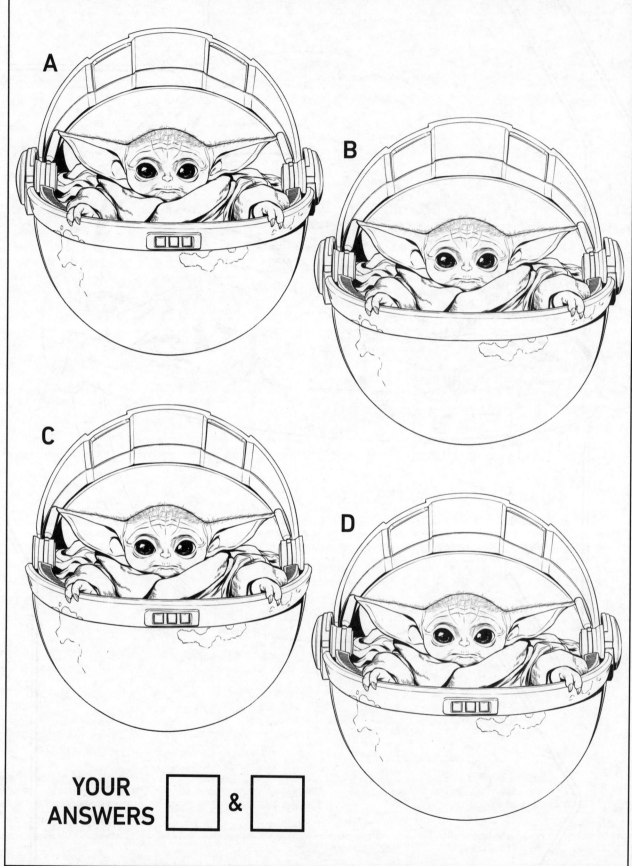

A

B

C

D

YOUR
ANSWERS [ ] & [ ]

Answers: A & D

WORD SCRAMBLE

Unscramble the letters to correctly spell the names and words.

ROGUG

_____

TEH RMORERA

_____

RUGB

_____

ETH DALOMANIANR

_____

The Mandalorian and Grogu.

The Urban Girl's Manifesto

Melody Biringer

CRAVE Calgary: The Urban Girl's Manifesto

A publication of The CRAVE Company
1805 12th Ave W #A
Seattle WA 98119
206.282.0173

thecravecompany.com/calgary
twitter.com/cravecalgary
facebook.com/cravecalgary

While every effort was made to ensure the accuracy of the information, details are subject to change so please call ahead. Neither The CRAVE Company nor CRAVE Calgary shall be responsible for any consequences arising from the publication or use.

All editorial content in this publication is the sole opinion of CRAVE Calgary and our contributing writers. No fees or services were rendered in exchange for inclusion in this publication.

Printed in the United States of America

ISBN 978-0-9847143-3-9
First Edition
December 2011
$19.95 USD

The Urban Girl's Manifesto

We CRAVE Community.

At CRAVE Calgary we believe in acknowledging, celebrating and passionately supporting local businesses. We know that, when encouraged to thrive, neighborhood establishments enhance communities and provide rich experiences not usually encountered in mass-market. By introducing you to the savvy businesswomen in this guide, we hope that CRAVE Calgary will help inspire your own inner entrepreneur.

We CRAVE Adventure.

We could all use a getaway, and at CRAVE Calgary we believe that you don't need to be a jet-setter to have a little adventure. There's so much to do and explore right in your own backyard. We encourage you to break your routine, to venture away from your regular haunts, to visit new businesses, to explore all the funky finds and surprising spots that Calgary has to offer. Whether it's to hunt for a birthday gift, indulge in a spa treatment, order a bouquet of flowers or connect with like-minded people, let CRAVE Calgary be your guide for a one-of-a-kind hometown adventure.

We CRAVE Quality.

CRAVE Calgary is all about quality products and thoughtful service. We know that a satisfying shopping trip requires more than a simple exchange of money for goods, and that a rejuvenating spa date entails more than a quick clip of the cuticles and a swipe of polish. We know you want to come away feeling uplifted, beautiful, excited, relaxed, relieved and, above all, knowing you got the most bang for your buck. We have scoured the city to find the hidden gems, new hot spots and old standbys, all with one thing in common: they're the best of the best!

A Guide to Our Guide

CRAVE Calgary is more than a guidebook. It's a savvy, quality-of-lifestyle book devoted entirely to local businesses owned by women. CRAVE Calgary will direct you to some of the best local spots—top boutiques, spas, cafés, stylists, fitness studios and more. And we'll introduce you to the inspired, dedicated women behind these exceptional enterprises, for whom creativity, quality, innovation and customer service are paramount.

Not only is CRAVE Calgary an intelligent guide for those wanting to know what's happening throughout town, it's a directory for those who value the contributions that spirited businesswomen make to our region.

Summit Kids

403.477.5437
summitkids.ca, Twitter: @summit_kids

Innovative. Fun. Enriching.
Summit Kids prides itself on offering cutting-edge out-of-school programming.
Not only do they provide a personalized service, trusted care and secure
centers, but they have also developed their program by building strong
relationships with various community resources. Summit Kids' extensive and
integrated program provides families with an array of options for wellness,
learning, creativity and social development with a focus on fun and safety.

Photos by Tara Whittaker Photography

Nancy E. Klensch

Q&A

What tip would you give women
who are starting a business?
Do what you love and love what you
do. Mostly, do what you're good at
and hire out for the rest. A great
team is the best support system.

What do you like best about
owning a business?
Having the ability and control to create
and re-create a world I want to live in.

What motivates you on a daily basis?
My son. He started me on this journey
and pushes me to want more. He's
relentless, rarely taking no for an answer—a
characteristic he shares with his mother!

What do you CRAVE?
Travel and food. Sand between my toes,
sun on my face and a warm tropical breeze.
Always, always, an exquisite glass of wine.

Evelyn L. Ackah

Q&A

What are your most popular
products or services?
Providing analysis and guidance to
obtain Canadian and U.S. work permits,
permanent residence status and work
permit and visas for employees.

What sets your business apart
from the competition?
We provide predictable, cost-effective
guidance through the entire immigration
process. Our innovative approach to client
management, alternative fee structures
and 24/7 access to our immigration team
is what makes our firm truly unique.

What is your motto or theme song?
"Our deepest fear is not that we are
inadequate. Our deepest fear is that
we are powerful beyond measure. It is
our light, not our darkness that most
frightens us." —Marianne Williamson

Ackah Business Immigration Law

Lord Denning House: 509 - 20th Ave SW, Calgary, 403.452.9515, 604.639.2146
ackahlaw.com, Twitter: @ackahlaw

Professional. Specialized. Effective.

Ackah Business Immigration Law believes that the practice of law is first and foremost about people. It is a boutique immigration law firm providing seamless client service, a personal commitment to building long-term professional relationships and specialized knowledge backed by years of legal experience. The Ackah Business Immigration Law team is pleased to share their passion for business immigration law with their clients all around the world.

Southwest

 # Q&A

Amy Johnston

What are your most popular
products or services?
In-home personal training and boot camps.

Who is your role model or mentor?
People who exude their passion. Success
is fulfilling your needs as a person and if
your passion is able to help others, I think
that is the greatest measure of success!

What is your motto or theme song?
Sometimes I say to clients, "If it
were easy, what would be the
point?" Also, "The time is now!"

What do you CRAVE?
Happiness, love, success and the high
of being able to love what I do!

Aim4fitness

403.617.6148, aim4fitness.net, Twitter: @aim4FitnessCAN

Energetic. Convenient. Personal.
Aim4fitness is a business dedicated to helping people achieve their overall health
and fitness goals. Their energetic personal training offers individuals the convenience
of working out in the comfort of your home. No equipment or travel is required, just
a small space and the willingness to commit. Aim4fitness promotes the belief that
investing in overall health and wellness is the key to longevity and happiness.

Alice (Aliki) Rathgeber

Q&A

What tip would you give women
who are starting a business?
Be mentored by those you respect. Don't
be afraid of mistakes or rejection. Both
will happen. As we say in art... a mistake
is just a new idea waiting to happen.

What do you like best about
owning a business?
I love having the freedom to change
what isn't working, to explore new
areas of interest and to creatively
direct the vision of the company.

What motivates you on a daily basis?
My love of watching what happens when
art enters someone's life—especially
people who consider themselves "non
artists." Watching people learn how
to play again just never gets old!

Aliki's Art House and Art in Mind

403.667.7020
AlikisArtHouse.com

Educational. Fun. Therapeutic.
Believing that anyone could be taught how to draw, Aliki's Art House endeavored to do just that. Aliki's has been teaching the foundational skill of drawing for over 20 years to hundreds of artists from beginners to professionals. Having witnessed the therapeutic effects of creating art, Aliki's added art as therapy to her repertoire. Aliki's hopes to expand into Australia in the near future.

Photos by Visual Hues Photography, except upper left and right photos by Kristi Sneddon

Anne Wright Photography

403.200.2158
annewrightphotography.com, Twitter: @AnneWrightPhoto

Intimate. Vibrant. Sincere.
Anne Wright is an international award-winning photographer who provides an extraordinary photographic experience to a discerning clientele. Given her natural enthusiasm and passionate creativity, it isn't surprising that Anne loves to capture people in love and children at play. Her sophisticated, vibrant style will appeal to those looking for something unique: a truly personal, timeless piece of art.

Anne Wright

 # Q&A

What are your most popular products or services?
Books that tell a rich, visual story. All my albums are handcrafted in New Zealand by the best in the business, making each of them an heirloom.

What tip would you give women who are starting a business?
Be realistic. They say it takes three years to be an overnight sensation. Therefore, be passionate and driven, work hard. But don't forget you have a family and friends...

What is your motto or theme song?
Luck is what happens when preparation meets opportunity.

Apex Massage Therapy

1167 Kensington Cres NW, Ste 314, Calgary, 403.270.7788
908 17th Ave SW, Ste 305, Calgary, 403.244.8925
apexmassage.com

Professional. Luxurious. Beneficial.
You deserve an Apex massage! Apex has been serving Calgary since 1994 and
has grown to two locations with 17 registered massage therapists. Both locations
will exceed your expectations. Experience one therapist or try them all.

Spagoes

403.521.2282, spagoes.ca

Relaxing. Attentive. Balancing.
Spagoes is a premier mobile spa, bringing the decadence and luxury of a resort spa to
your home. Their team offers a welcoming attitude that is hard to find anywhere else.

Photos by Jennifer Chipperfield Photography

Shelly MacGregor

Q&A

What are your most popular products or services?
We specialize in massage! Offering sports, therapeutic, relaxation, prenatal or postnatal, hot-stone massage or Thai massage, our well-educated team will treat specifically to your needs.

What tip would you give women who are starting a business?
Define the lifestyle you want and go after it! Being the boss can take over your life, make sure you know why you want to start a business.

What do you like best about owning a business?
I started as a massage therapist but have grown into other roles such as CEO, CFO, marketing director, HR consultant, etc. Learning and growing have endless possibilities.

Argento Creative

403.837.1931
argentocreative.com

Creative. Passionate. Dedicated.

Argento Creative design studio focuses on illuminating and understanding their clients' goals and dreams, and translating those into great design. By taking a personal interest in their clients, Argento Creative ensures that the final product matches each client's vision. Whether the client is a large corporation or a smaller, independent start-up, Argento Creative synthesizes superior graphic design with client vision for effective, impactful results.

 # Q&A

What are your most popular products or services?
Branding and identity packages, marketing pieces, brochures, self-promotion. My clients include larger companies and I also love working with small start-ups to assist them on their road to success.

What tip would you give women who are starting a business?
Don't give up, and be patient! And if you make a mistake, embrace it, learn from it and never make the same mistake again. Believe in yourself and your company.

What do you like best about owning a business?
I love the direct, one-on-one relationship-building with my clients. They become more than just a "project": I want them to succeed, and I take a personal interest in their goals.

Deneen Tedeschini

Tara Anand

Q&A

What are your most popular products or services?
Makeup Diploma Programs are the focus but we also hire out artists for photo shoots etc and have a boutique style modelling agency. In addition we offer personal lessons.

What inspires you and why?
Success inspires me. Making a difference to our students lives inspires me. They in turn inspire my vision and creativity and that is why I love what I do.

What do you CRAVE?
I'm excited for our new project in the works, an online makeup school. I'm thrilled we will be able to offer anyone, anywhere the opportunity to follow their dreams.

Artists Within Makeup Academy

306 - 822 11th Ave SW, Calgary, 403.208.0034
artistswithin.com, Twitter: @artistswithin

Creative. Stimulating. Compelling.
Artists Within is the first school in Calgary dedicated to instructing aspiring
makeup artists. It is Alberta's only makeup academy to offer accredited diploma
programs in Makeup, Hair Design, Advanced Makeup and Fashion Styling.
We are also connected with ITEC in London, England, allowing our students to
take an international exam, giving them certification recognized worldwide.

 # Q&A

Ava Czymoch

What tip would you give women
who are starting a business?
Resiliency! There are a lot of ups and
downs with starting a business, and
learning to roll with the punches will help
you get through those tough times.

What motivates you on a daily basis?
The feeling of knowing I can help
someone feel better about themselves.
Unleashing beauty is a powerful thing!

What is your motto or theme song?
Never a failure, always a lesson.

What place inspires you and why?
I love traveling to Europe and soaking
in the culture and lifestyle. They seem
to embody a passion for living life to the
fullest, and the fashion looks so effortless.

Beauty Uncovered

403.818.8262
beautyuncovered.ca, Twitter: @AvaUncovered

Stylish. Authentic. Savvy.
Whether it's updating your wardrobe, refreshing your makeup palette or finding
the perfect designer dress for a night on the town, Beauty Uncovered has you
covered. Servicing the Calgary area for three years, Beauty Uncovered specializes
in the art of transformation and helping women uncover their true beauty.

Jennifer Ruparell

Q&A

What are your most popular products or services?
Spa gift certificate (choice of four Spas including Oasis, Peel, RnR Wellness, and Health Span), chocolates, soy candles and natural beauty products.

What tip would you give women who are starting a business?
Stay true to your instincts and follow your dreams. Don't be afraid to take chances. You can fall seven times, but get up eight. Find mentors in your industry who care.

What motivates you on a daily basis?
My daughter Malia, who is my ray of sunshine. Through her rose-coloured glasses, life is simple and sweet. She has no fear and no inhibitions. I am learning daily.

BeautyGram Inc

403.702.4438
beautygram.ca, Twitter: @jennirups

Pampering. Chic. Convenient.
Forget flowers, send a BeautyGram! Sending a BeautyGram is an excellent
gift to treat those you care about in a simple and convenient way. Wrapped
in a little pink box and tied with a chic black ribbon, BeautyGram is the finest
beauty experience filled with all the must-haves women love—uniquely
packaged, tagged and delivered right to the woman you wish to pamper.

Sarah Bing

Q&A

What are your most popular
products or services?
Original oil-on-canvas paintings
principally influenced by the
Expressionism art movement.

What do you like best about
owning a business?
The process of working with clients from the
conceptualization of an idea to the finalized
and warmly received piece of artwork.

What is your biggest fear?
Painter's block...

What is your motto or theme song?
Shaping a dream to canvas.

What do you CRAVE?
To connect with others through art.

BING Art Studio

403.473.3337
sarahbing.com

Vibrant. Contemporary. Fluid.
Founder of BING Art Studio, Sarah Bing is one of Calgary's most vibrant
visual artists. Her fluid application of paint to canvas gives life to virtually
any subject matter. The imagery of expressed meaning and emotional
experience are captured passionately intertwined on one canvas.

breathe hot yoga

12445 Lake Fraser Dr SE, Ste 321, Calgary, 403.264.YOGA (403.264.9642)
breathehotyoga.ca, Twitter: @BreatheHotYoga

Warm. Inviting. Peaceful.
breathe hot yoga is south Calgary's premier hot yoga studio. From the minute you walk through the doors, your stresses melt away as you take in the spa-like upscale warmth and beauty. In addition to offering a wide variety of yoga styles taught by a team of amazing and unique instructors, breathe offers many extra special touches that will help you leave a little more "zen" than when you arrived.

breathe hot yoga

Suzie Allan

 # Q&A

What tip would you give women who are starting a business?
Follow your dreams and everything will fall into place. It's scary and it's hard, but it's so worth it.

What motivates you on a daily basis?
What motivates me are the people that tell me breathe has changed their lives. Could there be anything more rewarding or motivating than that?

How do you relax?
The minute I step into my hot room and I'm enveloped by the warmth and candlelight, I'm immediately relaxed. I feel blessed that my workplace is also my sanctuary.

Who inspires you and why?
The people who come to the studio. Seeing them grow and change is an inspiration to me every single day.

breathe life.
breathe love.
breathe peace.
breathe yoga

The Bridal Group
of Companies

839 - 10th Ave SW, Calgary, 403.229.3388
theweddingfair.ca, bridalexpo.ca, calgarybridalguide.com

Innovative. Creative. Passionate.
The Bridal Group is all about weddings! From producing premier wedding events,
to publishing Calgary's number one planning resource, from directing the Calgary
Bridal Association to creating a local wedding blog, The Bridal Group is passionate
about the industry and knows the importance of professionalism and integrity in the
marketplace. The Bridal Group is the definitive source for all things wedding.

Q&A

Lisa Vettese, Kathie James
and Lenora Kingcott

What are your most popular products or services?
The Wedding Fair, Bridal Expo, Calgary Bridal Guide, Calgary Bridal Association, Calgarybride.ca.

What tip would you give women who are starting a business?
Do your market research and ensure there is a need in the marketplace!

What place inspires you and why?
The trade show floor on the day of an event—watching the excitement and feeling the energy of the brides-to-be.

What is your motto or theme song?
"That's What Friends Are For."

What motivates you on a daily basis?
Seeing the success and creativity of our clients.

Mount Royal

Compassionate Beauty™

By appointment only: 26 - 22 Richard Way SW, Calgary, 403.686.6936
compassionatebeauty.com, Twitter: @CompassionateB

Nurturing. Understanding. Respectful.
Compassionate Beauty™ is a unique retail-service concept specifically
targeting women affected by cancer. The majority of treatment options, such as
chemotherapy and surgery, leave women feeling self-conscious and vulnerable.
Compassionate Beauty provides an extensive range of products and services
specifically designed and created to help manage the visual, physical and
psychological side effects of cancer treatment in a nonclinical, spa-like setting.

Saundra Shapiro

Q&A

What tip would you give women
who are starting a business?
You must be passionate about
your business, the concept and the
clients you want to serve. Commit
to five years of 110 percent effort
and be the best that you can be.

What motivates you on a daily basis?
Helping others. I am always so humbled
by the courage of women who are fighting
for their lives every day, enduring months
of chemotherapy, radiation and surgery.

What do you CRAVE?
A world without cancer.

Jodi Willoughby and
Carolyne McIntyre Jackson

Q&A

What are your most popular products or services?
The Crave-o-licious and Red Velvet cupcakes as well as chocolate chip cookies and always cakes!

What tip would you give women who are starting a business?
Love what you do; we are passionate about baking, and it shows in everything we do from the products that we test to tying the perfect bow on each package.

What do you like best about owning a business?
Working with each other and doing what we love and sharing it with others.

What do you CRAVE?
Fabulous, whole, natural foods including baked goods, of course.

Crave Cupcakes

1107 Kensington Rd NW, Calgary, 403.209.4903
222 - 10816 MacLeod Trail SE, Calgary, 403.278.3865
318 Aspen Glen Landing SW, Calgary, 403.221.8307
#57 Crowfoot Terrace NW, Calgary, 403.237.8486
Order Line: 403.270.2728
cravecupcakes.ca, Twitter: @craveyyc

Fun. Homemade. Delicious.

Crave Cupcakes began with a passion for baking. Inspired by fresh ingredients and family recipes, we learned the art of baking on our family farm in High River, Alberta, alongside our mother and grandmothers. Growing up in a busy kitchen inspired an appetite for simple, sweet indulgences made from scratch that led to the creation of Crave Cupcakes.

Michele Serpanchy

Q&A

What are your most popular products or services?
Primarily our service is daytime child care, but we are striving toward building a community centre atmosphere that encourages families to come for dinner and an evening activity as well.

What do you like best about owning a business?
Being the one to set the tone for the environment and quality of care that children receive. I would love to see a focus on early learning become standard practice.

What motivates you on a daily basis?
Enriching the daily life of my own children plus the other children who come to our centre every day is what motivates me to do more.

The Creative Tree Early Learning Centre Inc.

13 - 6325 12th St SE, Calgary, 403.453.1072
creativetree.ca, Twitter: @CreativeTreeInc

Bright. Inspiring. Cooperative.
The Creative Tree helps Calgary fulfill a need for quality child care. By taking the established fundamentals of child care and infusing elements of flexibility and innovation, they are able to offer an exceptional environment designed to enhance the development of each individual child and family. Options include traditional full-time care, evening and weekend family activities, drop-in services and a fully equipped health-inspired kitchen.

Paula Callihoo

Q&A

What tip would you give women who are starting a business?
I would say you have to be very passionate about your business in order to make it work. Passion helps you get through the hard times and keeps you focused.

What motivates you on a daily basis?
I'm motivated by wanting to help make a difference in someone's life. If someone comes into the studio and is inspired to get active, we have done our job.

What is your motto or theme song?
"I Hope You Dance" is a song I find very inspiring. I think it really says it all. You need to keep dancing no matter what challenges you face.

Dance Through Life

104 - 58 Ave SE, Calgary, 403.921.9757
dancethroughlife.ca

Active. Unique. Inspirational.
Dance Through Life is an adult dance and fitness studio that offers dance and
fitness classes to new beginners or experienced dancers of any age. Located
centrally near Chinook Mall, the studio opened in September of 2009. Dance
Through Life is committed to fun and fitness in a noncompetiitve environment. They
encourage everyone to come out, have fun, stay active and Dance Through Life!

Dashing Dishes Calgary

403.471.1395
dashingdishes.com

Convenient. Delicious. Healthy.

Dashing Dishes solves your mealtime dilemma. They do the planning, shopping, chopping and cleanup. In an hour, assemble a variety of meals to satisfy any family. Short on time? They can assemble meals for you! Menu items are family-friendly and change monthly, so you'll never get bored. Register online to attend a session near you and leave with a cooler full of delicious, healthy meals.

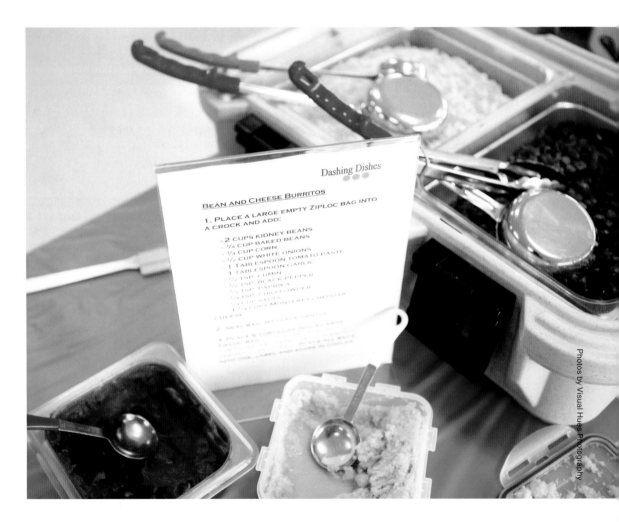

Nydia Hefflick

Q&A

What are your most popular products or services?
Our delicious ever-changing menu of ready-to-cook entreés ensure busy families enjoy healthy, homemade meals together night after night!

What tip would you give women who are starting a business?
Take the time to plan and don't be afraid to take risks.

What is your motto or theme song?
What you think about, you bring about.

What place inspires you and why?
I always feel a sense of motivation, inspiration and gratitude when I visit new countries.

doo-dads

2133 - 33rd Ave SW, Calgary, 403.240.3033

Welcoming. Imaginative. Captivating.

Entering doo-dads evokes the wonder of a 1920s Paris atelier. Old-world drafting tables are bursting with fresh fashion jewellery. Antique French library shelves are filled with purses, accessories and ingenious gift pieces. Add in the classical music and warm greetings from the counter, and every visit is sure to be *très* delightful.

Dale O'Quinn

 # Q&A

What do you like best about owning a business?
I have the wonderful opportunity to do what I love doing and to share my passion with customers every day.

What are your most popular products or services?
The tremendous, ever-changing variety of well-priced fashion pieces at doo-dads ensures visitors will always enjoy new and exciting discoveries.

What is your motto or theme song?
"Carpe diem!" Seize the day and give it your all!

What place inspires you and why?
In the evenings, I enjoy sitting at a lovely, old desk in my office. It's heaped with family photos and memorabilia that warm my heart.

Marda Loop

Elevated HR Solutions

By appointment only: 604 27th Ave NE, Calgary, 403.277.2844
elevatedhr.com, Twitter: @elevatedhr

Renegade. No-nonsense. Solution-oriented.
Elevated HR Solutions (EHR) is on a mission to take HR out of the business. Solutions
are developed that actually work for start-ups and small businesses. EHR develops
programs and initiatives customized to each organization and understands the importance
of increasing the bottom line. Elevated HR currently services North America—with clients
located in Alberta, British Columbia, Manitoba and throughout the United States.

Photos by Erin Wallace Photography

Michelle Berg

Q&A

What are your most popular products or services?
Human resources support, programs and ideas as they relate to attracting, engaging and retaining staff.

What tip would you give women who are starting a business?
Perfection of a business plan is not the only thing you need to start a business—it's the *execution* of the plan.

What do you like best about owning a business?
I am building a legacy that I can call my own.

What motivates you on a daily basis?
The fact that we are truly making a difference with the services we provide.

What is your motto or theme song?
Stop worrying about making money, and just make magic.

What place inspires you and why?
Anyplace that has like-minded individuals who are out to not only make a difference, but win. I love a competitive vibe.

What do you CRAVE?
The opportunity to build a massive company internationally.

Susan Elford

Q&A

What are your most popular products or services?
People repeatedly come to me for my strategic communications planning and media relations services. My clients tell me they like how I am able to integrate myself into their team and truly understand their organization's goals.

What tip would you give women who are starting a business?
Be patient. Get networked. Word hard. You will be amazed at how successful you can be when you put your mind to it!

What do you like best about owning a business?
I love the autonomy, flexibility and diversity of offering communications services to a range of clients.

Elford Communications

1304 Kelowna Cres SW, Calgary, 403.830.1471
elfordcommunications.com, Twitter: @susanelford

Strategic. Collaborative. Effective.
Every organization has a story to tell. Elford Communications helps
organizations understand their unique story or brand and build those stories
into effective communications strategies that deliver results. Susan Elford
has been helping organizations achieve their business objectives through
effective communications since 1992. With experience in corporate, not-for-
profit and government sectors, Susan brings her strong consulting skills to
the table through strategic communications planning, issues management,
media relations, writing, project management and special event planning.

Photos by Jennifer Chipperfield Photography

Brittany Geschwendt

Q&A

What are your most popular products or services?
The Redefined Body Nutrition Program, a 28-day program to reset your blood glucose levels so that your body functions at its optimum level. Also, Nurse Navigator is great for women wanting personal guidance and coaching.

What do you like best about owning a business?
I love the ability to design a nutrition program. The content, colors and style I use on my website are exactly what I envisioned it to be. My creative side can flourish!

What motivates you on a daily basis?
My passion for women's health and my own dreams inspire me to be courageous in living a life of wellbeing and empower other women to do the same.

Embrace Wellbeing

403.463.2214
embracewellbeing.ca, Twitter: @britgeschwendt

Genuine. Inspiring. Passionate.
Embrace Wellbeing inspires women to choose a life that integrates wellness through nutrition programs, advice and incredible encouragement. These programs are for every woman who yearns to change her life as well as specific programs for pre- and postnatal women. There's a section for personal/private guidance for women who want detailed steps to achieve a life of wellbeing. All programs are offered conveniently online.

The Skoop photographed by
SDS Creative and Inspire Studios

How do you relax?

"With a glass of wine, good friends and great conversation, the hours seem like minutes."

Michele Beitel of The Skoop

Erin Wallace

⬛Q&A

What are your most popular products or services?
The most popular services my business provides are portrait, editorial, event and product photography.

What do you like best about owning a business?
What I like best about owning a business is the diversity in my day and the fascinating people I have the honour of working with.

Who is your role model or mentor?
My mentors are wonderful artists, photographers, filmmakers and entrepreneurs; my parents Murray and Karin Wallace, Roger Vernon, John Barth, Craig Richards, Jason Stang, Kate Kunz and Mary Ellen Mark.

Erin Wallace Photography

403.998.2510
erinwallacephotography.com, Twitter: @erinewallace

Intuitive. Revealing. Warm.
Erin Wallace Photography is a commercial photography business balanced with self-directed fine art and documentary assignments. Whether creating a portrait, photographing a wedding, documenting a human-interest story or creating traditional black-and-white prints, a sense of light, beauty and connection to her subject is present throughout Erin's work. Intuitive and deeply considered, Erin Wallace Photography is dedicated to creating engaging and revealing imagery.

Photos by Erin Wallace Photography

Estilo Home

403.998.9557
estilo.home@yahoo.com

Transforming. Harmonious. Essential.
Estilo Home is a reflection of Maria's passion for an organized and harmonious environment where order and beauty meet. She has an innate ability to transform every room in your home by simply organizing and working with what you have, and if she feels there is a need for some extra accessories, she will find the right pieces you will love, at the perfect price.

Q&A

What are your most popular products or services?
I have the expertise in transforming and face-lifting every area of your home without having to spend a lot of money, starting with organizing!

Who is your role model or mentor?
My role model and mentor is definitely my mother. She has always kept a beautiful home where everything has its place, and style is evident in the simplest ways. She taught me from an early age the importance of organization and the concept of creating beauty no matter how big or how small your budget.

How do you relax?
By simply living in the environment that I have created in my own home.

Maria Beatriz Galano-Maughan

Evolutions School of Dance

2633 Hochwald Ave SW, Calgary, 403.819.0758
evolutionsdance.com, Twitter: @evolutionsdance

Positive. Innovative. Inviting.

Evolutions School of Dance (ESD) is a centrally located dance school offering exciting classes in a variety of genres for dancers ages 2 to adult, from ballet to hip-hop to Ukrainian dance and more! Owned and administered by sisters (who are also school teachers), ESD's goal is to provide their dance students with an exceptional dance education, while becoming strong, confident and accomplished dancers.

Photos by Jennifer Chatterfield Photography

Vanessa Lewis, Natalka Lewis
and Stephanie Knowler

Q&A

What are your most popular products or services?
We are incredibly proud of our foundational preschool dance program, which is child-centred, educational, vibrant and exciting for all! These classes seem to be the most popular!

What tip would you give women who are starting a business?
We are so lucky to have each other for support. Ultimately, perseverance and determination have helped us—oh, and to learn from your mistakes and smile through it all!

What do you like best about owning a business?
Not only do we enjoy getting to know our amazing students and their families, we are also proud that we have created something together as sisters from the ground up!

Southwest

Ellinor Stenroos

 Q&A

What tip would you give women who are starting a business?
Let your clients see your passion; focus on showcasing what makes your love for your work infectious. Don't waste time on things that prevent you from doing your best.

What do you like best about owning a business?
I love the creative freedom and being able to develop designs and products that do not conflict with my aesthetics and quality requirements.

Who is your role model or mentor?
I admire a lot of European jewellery designers and silversmiths, particularly David Clarke in the United Kingdom and Atelier Verstraeten of Belgium.

EVStenroos

403.618.1781, evstenroos.com, Twitter: @evstenroos
Exhibited at Dade Art & Design Lab: 1327 9th Ave SE, Calgary, 403.454.0243
dadegallery.com, Twitter: @dadegallery

Contemporary. Bespoke. Minimalist.
Behind EVStenroos is designer Ellinor Stenroos, classically trained jeweller,
silver– and goldsmith based in Calgary. Ellinor was born in Finland and
trained in the United Kingdom. She works in Scandinavian design, creating
custom high-end jewellery, objects of art and functional sterling silver
pieces using clean lines and a contemporary aesthetic, without losing
the decadent appeal of a truly luxurious custom-made piece of art.

Kim Chernow-Little

Q&A

What are your most popular
products or services?
A variety of smaller-production
wines. We hold tasting events—from
corporate parties to sit-down birthday
dinners. Our Explore Wine Club offers
door-to-door delivery service.

What tip would you give women
who are starting a business?
Do what you are passionate about and your
business will explode! Learn as much as
you can about marketing and social media.
Survey and research your target market.

What do you like best about
owning a business?
I love having the freedom to make my
own decisions. When everything is based
on my creativity, my passions and my
ideas, my successes are truly my own.

The Ferocious Grape

833 10th Ave SW, Calgary, 403.457.0099
ferociousgrape.com, Twitter: @ferocious_grape

Relaxed. Friendly. Knowledgeable.
When it comes to buying wine at The Ferocious Grape, the only rule is there are no rules. Since opening in December of 2008, this wine boutique has been endeavoring to remove the pretension from the wine-shopping experience. Whether looking for the perfect bottle to live it up or to unwind, the informed staff will help you find exactly what you're after.

Photos by Erin Wallace Photography.

Design District

"The Fire Within" Acupuncture and Wellness

403.808.3427
thefirewithinacupuncture.com, Twitter: @FireAcupuncture

Life-changing. Empowering. Healing.
The Fire Within takes men and women alike on a journey of self-discovery: "Who I am," "Why am I here," "What is my inner calling?" They help clients rediscover and connect with the deepest parts of themselves, in a most unique and powerful way. Clients will heal themselves with guidance and become empowered from the inner strength they've achieved to the path of enlightenment and self-fulfillment.

 # Q&A

What tip would you give women who are starting a business?
Breathe, and keep walking. I imagined myself on a tightrope moving through the fog. Though I couldn't see ahead, below, or behind me, I just knew to keep moving forward.

Who is your role model or mentor?
My loving grandparents. On their farm I listened to them talk about which herbs they were taking and why. They showed me how to heal myself; I was inspired.

What is your motto or theme song?
"What lies behind us and what lies before us are tiny matters compared to what lies within us." —Ralph Waldo Emerson. This powerful quote speaks volumes for Spiritual empowerment.

Dr. Tanya Hartz

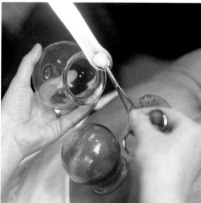

First Step Nutrition

403.608.3240
firststepnutrition.com, Twitter: @firststepnut

Professional. Passionate. Nourishing.
First Step Nutrition can help nourish your growing family with confidence! Jennifer House is a registered dietitian and specializes in nutrition for new moms, moms-to-be, babies and children. Jen helps her clients give their children the best nutritional start and teaches them how to have more peaceful and nutritious family meals.

Jennifer House

Q&A

What are your most popular products or services?
The grocery store tour is always a favorite. It is so practical to get in the grocery store and compare labels and products. That is where healthy choices start!

What motivates you on a daily basis?
I love working with pregnant women, as they are full of motivation and anticipation! Helping moms raise healthy families is very fulfilling.

What place inspires you and why?
Farmers markets inspire me to get back to the basics in preparing food. Delicious fresh produce, handmade multigrain bread, local meat and eggs, and meeting the farmers... love it!

Sarah Mayerson

Q&A

What are your most popular
products or services?
Wedding flowers with a focus on the
bridal bouquet, fresh European-style
hand-tied bouquets, gorgeous vase
arrangements, and unique one-of-a-kind
handmade jewelry by Calgary artists.

What tip would you give women
who are starting a business?
Stay true to yourself! It's difficult not
to compare yourself to your peers,
but ensuring that your business is a
reflection of you is essential to success.

What do you like best about
owning a business?
Having full creative ownership over all
aspects of my business, from branding
and marketing to which products are
brought in. I also enjoy the flexibility
to make my own schedule.

Flora

902 Edmonton Trail NE, Calgary, 403.457.1175
floracalgary.com, Twitter: @FloraCalgary

Sarah Mayerson Design

408 - 8th Ave NE, Calgary, 403.862.2242
sarahmayerson.com, Twitter: @smayersondesign

Fresh. Cutting-edge. Inspired.
Sarah Mayerson Design specializes in floral art for weddings and events. European-trained, Sarah has a natural eye for color and form, and strives to create breathtaking designs to reflect her clients' personal style. Sarah brings her passion for flowers to Flora, a lovely boutique flower shop located in Bridgeland. Offering lush floral arrangements, unique gifts and home decor and handmade products by local artists.

Photos by Tara Whittaker Photography

Bridgeland

Neelam Gurm

Q & A

What tip would you give women who are starting a business?
Believe in yourself!

What do you like best about owning a business?
The creativity and freedom it affords.

What motivates you on a daily basis?
All of our clients who have transformed their health and wellness with Fresh Cleanse!

What place inspires you and why?
Book stores: I love books! Learning, expanding and questioning the way I think, traveling to far-off places and making friends with people from different times and experiences.

What do you CRAVE?
Good food, good wine and good company.

Fresh Cleanse

403.969.2461
freshcleanse.ca, Twitter: @myfreshcleanse

Nurturing. Inspiring. Creative.
Fresh Cleanse is a nutritional juice cleanse delivered to your door! They use local and organic produce whenever possible to create beautiful gently squeezed juices that are never frozen, pasteurized or preserved. Simply replace your regular meals with their delicious juices and hit the reset button. Enjoy increased energy, better health and a happier, more vibrant you!

Fresh Start Yoga

403.243.4361
freshstartyoga.ca

Energizing. Grounding. Authentic.

With two decades of yoga experience, Fresh Start Yoga instructs in such a way that by simply attending classes you become your own best teacher. In community and corporate settings, Janice Piet offers a program that is tailored to mature body types. Through posture modifications, insightful observations and one-on-one dialogue, her aim is to create a truly personal experience in a group setting.

 # Q&A

What are your most popular products or services?

The final posture, Shivassana. I have a melt-in-your-mat guided meditation. My easy-to-follow audio CD is extremely popular.

What tip would you give women who are starting a business?

Start small. I began teaching classes in my home until we outgrew the space. Now I use my home space for private instruction or small-group teacher training.

What do you CRAVE?

Long drives through the mountains with my husband, Cort. A picnic basket filled with a whole roasted chicken, garlic-stuffed olives, bean medley salad, with ambrosia and dark chocolate for dessert.

Janice Piet

Gemma Stone

Q&A

What are your most popular products or services?
One-on-one intensive sessions are the most popular. They are designed to rewire ancient beliefs, heal past emotional wounds, mend damaging thoughts and firmly establish new habits to spark personal transformation.

What do you like best about owning a business?
Making a meaningful difference in the lives of my clients. Supporting my family to live their dreams. Being self-reliant, my success is a direct reflection of how much I contribute.

What place inspires you and why?
The West Coast Trail. I hiked it alone. Amid the challenge, exhaustion and pain, there was great peace. I found an inner strength I didn't know I had.

Gemma Stone International Inc.

403.255.0898
gemmastone.org, Twitter: @Gemma_Stone

Transformative. Comfortable. Positive.
Gemma Stone is a psychologist who is dedicated to empowering women to live happy, healthy and successful lives. She works with women who feel stuck, depressed, anxious, empty, fearful, unfulfilled or overwhelmed. Gemma fights for you with unconditional love and compassion. She combines the science of psychology with the power of spirituality to guide women through the process of making meaningful long-term change.

Photos by Tara Whittaker Photography

GirlPower

403.228.4107
urstrong.com, Twitter: @urstrong

Fun. Empowering. Cool.
GirlPower is a friendship program that inspires "tween" girls to feel empowered and love themselves while learning to manage the most important thing to them: their friendships. Girls learn the basics of creating and maintaining healthy relationships and how to stand up for themselves. GirlPower offers a fun six-week program and two-hour workshops, available for other educators to purchase and deliver to their own special girls!

 # Q&A

What are your most popular products or services?
The Six-Week Program. Along with role-playing, quizzes and artsy projects, girls are given fun weekly homework assignments. This program covers it all, leaving girls feeling inspired, empowered and more confident.

What tip would you give women who are starting a business?
Go for it! Follow your passion and create a business that's a true reflection of who you are and what you believe in. I promise it won't feel like work.

What place inspires you and why?
I can't help but feel inspired when I walk into a classroom... Kids are so full of life and excited to learn, create and explore!

Dana Kerford

Nichole Menard

 # Q&A

What tip would you give women who are starting a business?
Baby steps, move slowly even when your business is hot. Build a strong support network; we all need someone to lean on even during the good times.

What do you like best about owning a business?
Meeting new people daily and hearing their incredible life stories. Seeing the joy in a child's eyes when they gaze into our playroom. Lastly, bringing wonderful experiences to our customers.

What motivates you on a daily basis?
All the children running into our store, so excited to be in a place where they are honoured and respected.

gravity kidz

17 - 4307 130th Ave SE, Calgary, 403.257.5973
gravitykidz.ca

Inspiring. Ethical. Fun.

Gravity Kidz is a place where all children shine, and everyone feels at home. With unique, edgy clothing for children up to size 16 as well as engaging, educational toys and craft sets that spark creativity and imagination. The playroom and children's programs are fun for all ages. Gravity Kidz truly is a one-of-a-kind lifestyle store.

Green Way Packers

403.689.7663
greenwaypackers.net, Twitter: @greenwaypackers

Professional. Stress-free. Dependable.
Green Way Packers, winner of the 2011 Chamber of Commerce Service Excellence Awards, is your answer to getting ready for moving day. These all-women teams of home packers expertly and efficiently get household possessions wrapped, packed and sealed, ready for a move, renovation, downsize or storage. With an eco-friendly rebate program, local low-income seniors needing various services benefit directly from free recycled supplies.

Caryl Walker and Deb Darbyshire

Q&A

What tip would you give women
who are starting a business?
Never give up on a dream. Never tire of
the effort you put into your venture or
compromise on quality and service.

What do you like best about
owning a business?
Despite the amount of hours that go
into owning a business, the pride of
workmanship coupled with the flexibility
and having direct responsibility to our
customers make it all worthwhile.

What motivates you on a daily basis?
Knowing that the stressed homeowners
we see in the morning are relaxed and
calm by the end of an afternoon.

What is your motto or theme song?
If you're on the move, we're here to help!

Angela Schroeder

 # Q&A

What are your most popular products or services?

The look that started Haute Tots is one that fans always return to. The Haute Classic line includes Haute Chocolate, Haute Crème and Haute Pink, which are top sellers each season.

What tip would you give women who are starting a business?

Be authentic and genuine. Find what you truly feel connected to instead of trying to re-create what is currently thriving. Success will come to you for your unique vision.

What do you like best about owning a business?

I love that my work is also my creative outlet. I get to research fashion and design haute looks with no limits put on my creative vision.

Haute Tots

403.807.9169
hautetots.ca, Twitter: @hautetots

Archetypal. Classic. Authentic.
Haute Tots creates premium, fashion-forward crocheted hats in a multitude of styles and colours for children of all ages. Fans love their distinct vintage styling and retro-chic feel. They are the softest, most comfortable hats that you can find. Haute Tots are sure to become the go-to hat for your children as well as a must-have keepsake baby gift!

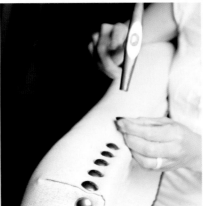

Melanie Jacober

Q&A

What are your most popular
products or services?
Upholstered headboards of course!

What tip would you give women
who are starting a business?
Believe in yourself and start by setting
small attainable goals; as you achieve
these, it will give you the momentum and
confidence to set and achieve bigger goals.

Who is your role model or mentor?
My Father: he has taught me so much
about life and business. He set up his
own company at age 18, and so he
has a wealth of knowledge to give.

What is your motto or theme song?
Laughter is the best medicine for life!

Head of the Bed

403.805.1474
headofthebed.ca

Custom. Dramatic. Luxurious.
Head of the Bed was created with a simple goal in mind: to transform bedrooms
from blah to beautiful, drab to dramatic in a cost-effective way. Head of the
Bed creates and designs headboards and matching accessories for children
and adult bedrooms. Clients are offered a one-on-one design consultation in
their homes to ensure the realization of their dreams for bedroom design.

All except main photo by Visual Hues Photography

Healthy Vending Calgary

403.852.0953
healthyvendingcalgary.com

Innovative. Educational. Inspiring.
Healthy Vending Calgary was created in response to a demand for healthy snack alternatives in our fast-paced lives. Healthy snacks should be easily accessible in our schools, offices and fitness centres. Healthy Vending is committed to changing the way people eat, and the way they think about what they eat. Products will never contain high fructose corn syrup, trans fats or artificial flavours.

Carolyn Horwitz

Q&A

What are your most popular products or services?
CheeCha Puffs, made in Calgary. They are potato flour, which is compressed, then put through a hot-air popper. They are an awesome crunchy snack without the guilt!

What tip would you give women who are starting a business?
Make sure you are passionate about what you do as you need to live and breathe it every single minute of every single day.

What do you like best about owning a business?
The freedom to make my own decisions and having to live with the consequences.

What is your biggest fear?
Not having enough time to change the world.

Jelly modern doughnuts

100, 1414 - 8 Street SW, Calgary, 403.453.2053
jellymoderndoughnuts.com, Twitter: @jellymodern

Fresh. Gourmet. Organic.

Jelly modern doughnuts is Canada's original gourmet doughnut bakery cafe. Their delicious doughnuts are uniquely handcrafted by talented pastry chefs and bakers, made fresh on-site every day. They use only the finest quality ingredients in their recipes and locally sourced and organic products are used whenever possible. A healthier artisan treat and a sophisticated update on a classic Canadian tradition.

Main and upper left and right photos by Ryan A. Monson, portrait and upper middle photo by Brian Harder

Rita and Rosanne Tripathy

Q&A

What are your most popular products or services?
The maple bacon hand filled doughnut and s'mores doughnuts have been our best sellers. Birthday parties, doughnut dipping parties and weddings are our most popular events.

What tip would you give women who are starting a business?
Choose a business you are passionate about and never compromise your vision.

What motivates you on a daily basis?
Striving to have everyone who consumes our doughnuts to have a beautiful experience. From the time they walk in the bakery until they unwrap the beautiful box and bite into their delectable treats.

Jennifer Chipperfield

Q&A

What are your most popular products or services?
Fantabulous custom-painted portraits, blingy Pretty Girl paintings and mixed media creations with amazing vintage ephemera.

What motivates you on a daily basis?
To express the creativity that sings in my veins and connect with the people I love through it.

How do you relax?
Tearing up strips of paper, smearing paint onto a canvas with my fingers, eating popcorn, dribbling ink with abandon, walking with my dogs.

What do you CRAVE?
Time and space to just be. To have enough downtime to really allow myself to be still—and then to experience and manifest the surge of creativity that comes from it.

Jennifer Chipperfield

403.263.6166
jenchipperfield.com, Twitter: @ChipPhoto

Creative. Connected. Fun.

Jennifer Chipperfield has been an innovative, well-known photographer in Calgary for many moons. Her passion for fine art has always been prevalent in her work, and her recently launched Mixed Media paintings and Pretty Girl portraits are an alternate side to Chipperfield Photography. Now anything is truly possible when it comes to creative ideas, images and design!

Photos by Jennifer Chipperfield Photography

Q&A

What are your most popular products or services?
Clients hire me because they have a particularly challenging goal they want to accomplish. My ENERGY to Thrive™ peak performance program is exactly what they need to make it happen.

What motivates you on a daily basis?
Seeing my clients striving to reach their peak potential and the satisfaction they experience when they push past their own self-created limitations to do something they thought wasn't possible.

What is your motto or theme song?
"Mens sana in corpore sano." —Latin for "a sound mind in a healthy body," which is the foundation for building an incredible life.

Jennifer Powter

Jennifer Powter

403.992.5367
jenniferpowter.com, Twitter: @jenpowter

Transformative. Energizing. Daring.

Jen Powter is one of Calgary's most popular performance coaches. Mother of two, Jen is an exercise physiologist and former wildland firefighter who used to spend her summers rappelling out of helicopters. A two-time Ironman finisher and experienced marathoner, these days you can find Jen running the trails with her clients while she helps them push past physical and emotional obstacles and reshape their lives.

Kathryn Aston Interiors

403.399.9313
kathrynastoninteriors.com

Creative. Client-focused. Knowledgeable.

Kathryn Aston Interiors is a full-service window treatment design business providing a fabulous range of custom blinds, shading solutions and drapery. Kathryn has years of experience and extensive product knowledge and is well recognized for her quality service. Focused on her clients' needs and preferences, she offers the latest in style and automated systems. She also offers custom soft furnishings.

Kathryn Aston

Q&A

What tip would you give women who are starting a business?
It's all about building relationships. Customer service and loyalty created by putting my clients' needs first have led to the majority of my new projects coming from referrals.

Who is your role model or mentor?
Audrey Hepburn. I love her sense of style and her humanity. She exudes classic beauty and a great sense of fun. She's elegant, timeless and selfless.

What is your motto?
Measure twice, cut once. I am very detail-oriented and it is extremely important to me to do it right the first time.

Kay Phair Advising

403.512.1978
kayphair.com, Twitter: @kayphair

Real. Compelling. Inspired.
Kay Phair Advising provides interesting, compelling and relevant copywriting
for businesses. No matter the topic, no matter the industry, owner Kelly Ferrier
captures the appropriate voice to speak to your target audience and compel them
to action. Writing services include website copywriting, including SEO; marketing
materials, including annual reports, magazine articles, brochures; grant applications;
social media and blog posts; profiles; advertising; and press releases.

Photos by Jennifer Chipperfield Photography

Kelly Ferrier

Q&A

What tip would you give women who are starting a business?
Trust your intuition above all. And if there's one word to remember first and foremost, it's *balance*—take time for yourself!

What do you like best about owning a business?
I love the flexibility and the variety. I get to meet and work with amazing people in a wide variety of industries, and I'm always learning new things.

What place inspires you and why?
The mountains—they're beautiful but also strong. And that's an apt description of what it means to be a female entrepreneur.

What do you CRAVE?
Relationships with energetic, inspiring and kind people. Opportunities to learn and grow.

Ki-Stone Wellness Inc.

403.667.3556
key2calm.com, Twitter: @key2calm

Restorative. Informative. Calming.
Ki-Stone Wellness Inc. is driven by the understanding that health is the ultimate wealth. Through kinesthetic self-care workshops, complementary care sessions in the form of Reflexology and Reiki (R&R), an informative speaker series, a bounty of articles, classes and more... Ki-Stone invites their clientele to learn how to thrive during their own discovery and achievement of personal health goals and successes.

Monique DeNault

 Q&A

What do you like best about owning a business?
Waking up every morning to a job I am truly passionate about. So many opportunities to make a difference and be the change I want to see in the world.

What motivates you on a daily basis?
The excited or relieved look on my clients faces when they start understanding the role they play in their own well being and begin to feel the results.

What is your motto or theme song?
Health is the ultimate wealth. Without it we really have nothing.

What place inspires you and why?
My home, because I get to use each space to create my perfect sanctuary.

Summit Kids photographed by Tara Whittaker Photography

What motivates you on a daily basis?

" *My son. He started me on this journey and pushes me to want more. He's relentless, rarely taking no for an answer—a characteristic he shares with his mother!* "

Nancy E. Klensch of Summit Kids

Kristi Sneddon

Q&A

What do you like best about owning a business?
The freedom to create. Thinking outside the box.

Who is your role model or mentor?
My family and friends. I'm very lucky to be surrounded by fantastic people, and they inspire me.

What motivates you on a daily basis?
My children!

What is your motto or theme song?
Live with intention. Walk to the edge. Listen hard. Practice wellness. Play with abandon. Laugh. Continue to learn. Appreciate your friends. Do what you love.

Kristi Sneddon Photographer

403.835.3055
ksphotographer.com, Twitter: @ksneddon

Sophisticated. Romantic. Extraordinary.
Kristi Sneddon is a people photographer. She loves to capture the true essence of people. She will make you feel special and unique (because you are). The resulting photographs will reflect your personality and all the wonderful things you are. Her attention to detail and customer satisfaction are key to her success. Kristi Sneddon is photography for the sophisticated romantic.

Photos by Kristi Sneddon

Lauren Lane Decor

4020 - 15A St SE, Calgary, 403.265.7751
lldecor.ca, Twitter: @lldecor

Vintage. Salvage. Inspired.
If you're looking for an inspired, personal touch to add to your home, Lauren
Lane Decor holds the key. With care and creativity, Lauren Lane Decor
will take treasured pieces—or pieces that are sure to become so—and
reimagine them for your space. From antique and dreamy to vibrant and
energetic, your interiors will get just the right touch from Lauren Lane.

Photos by Jennifer Chipperfield Photography

Tara Jamieson

Q&A

What are your most popular products or services?
Lauren Lane offers classes for DIYers looking to get their hands dirty as well as a custom refinishing process that will give you exactly the look you're after.

What tip would you give women who are starting a business?
Plan for success! With hard work and a bit of planning, it will happen. Don't get taken by surprise—make sure you're ready for the future when it happens!

What motivates you on a daily basis?
A lot of people are looking for "authentic"— they want something real and personal to them in their homes. That kind of work is really gratifying and very inspiring.

 # Q&A

What are your most popular products or services?
People can see, smell and feel the quality that organic French lavender and bamboo material have in our products, including our most popular: heating pads, dryer sachets and essential oils.

What tip would you give women who are starting a business?
Start small. Bigger is not necessarily better. Word of mouth, markets and social media are the best ways to promote a business without spending a fortune.

What place inspires you and why?
France. An amazing year spent there with my husband... the pace of life, amazing food, culture and time spent with family and friends are memories that still inspire me.

Michelle Forbes

Lavender Breeze
The Lavender Shoppe

lavenderbreeze.ca, Twitter: @lavender_breeze

Relaxing. Luxurious. Organic.

Lavender Breeze's organic, eco-friendly products fill a need for natural, safe products. High-quality, pure organic lavender and lavender essential oils imported from France fill their products with the healing qualities of the same lavender that has been growing wild in France for hundreds of years. Bamboo material adds a luxurious touch to their products, which can be found online, at farmers markets and in stores around Calgary.

Lifestyles
Wellness Group

403.247.9301
drformoms.com

Unique. Inspiring. Mission-driven.
Dr. Patricia Hort has devoted her chiropractic practice to the care of women from fertility through life with baby. Her signature treatment care programs—Back to Basics Baby Making, How to Have a Baby in Six Hours or Less and Get Your Body Back— guide moms-to-be through natural fertility, comfortable pregnancies and shorter labours, and supports them with strength and inspiration to thrive in momhood.

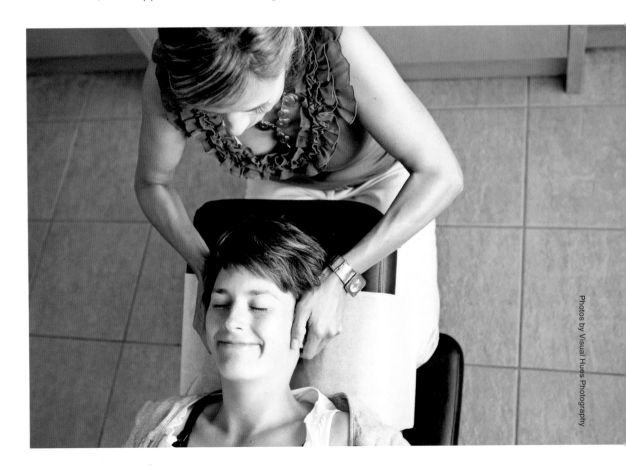

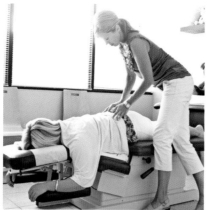

Dr. Patti Hort

Q&A

What are your most popular
products or services?
Dr. Hort and her multidisciplinary team
of natural healthcare providers offer
unique care programs for natural fertility,
sciatica, back/pelvic pain, pelvic floor
recovery, plagiocephaly and torticollis.
Oh yeah, there's childcare too!

What tip would you give women
who are starting a business?
Passionately love what you do and
think bigger about who you are and
what you offer those you serve.

What do you like best about
owning a business?
The creativity and personal expression;
the striving for excellence in fulfilling
a mission on your own terms.

Sally Lloyd

Q&A

**What are your most popular
products or services?**
Dental cleanings in our relaxed atmosphere,
followed by our professional teeth whitening
services and custom sports mouth guards.

**What tip would you give women
who are starting a business?**
Try to shadow someone who is already
doing what you want to do. You don't have
to reinvent the wheel, just make it better!

**What do you like best about
owning a business?**
I enjoy having input in my daily schedule,
ensuring my work, family and personal
time is balanced for me. That makes
for a happy, healthy dental hygienist!

Lifetime Smiles Dental Hygiene Clinic

11150 Bonaventure Dr SE, Ste 204, Calgary, 403.457.2044
lifetimesmiles.ca, Twitter: @lifetimesmileDH

Modern. Relaxing. Unique.

Sally Lloyd is owner and one of the practicing dental hygienists at Lifetime Smiles Dental Hygiene Clinic, located inside Trico Centre for Family Wellness in Southeast Calgary. Redefining the manner in which traditional dental hygiene care is provided, the clinic's hygienists extend to clients the benefits of this progressive oral health-care concept. Choose your dental hygienist and discuss your individual dental health-care needs.

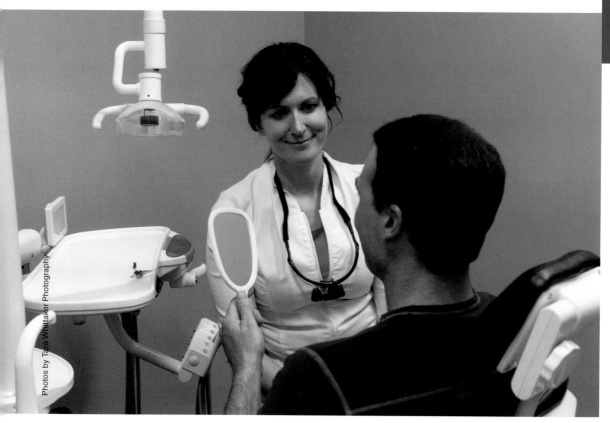

Photos by Tara Whittaker Photography

Nikki Shibou

 # Q&A

What tip would you give women
who are starting a business?
I think it's essential to have a solid
business plan. It's never wise to wing it!
Never override your gut instinct. I always
trust my gut; it's never been wrong.

What do you like best about
owning a business?
I love that I'm able to use every part of my
mind in all aspects of my business. I'm
the bookkeeper, the marketing person,
the employee... I've never been bored!

What motivates you on a daily basis?
I love being able to make a difference in the
lives of my clients. It's incredibly rewarding
to share the successes of treatment—
it's life changing for many people.

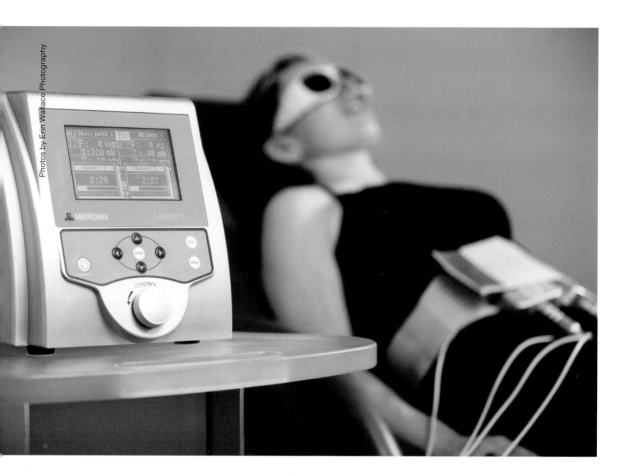

Lipolaser Solutions

By appointment only: 6036 3rd St SW, Ste 104, Calgary, 403.452.9622
lipolasersolutions.com

Life-altering. Empowering. Motivational.
Lipolaser Solutions provides a safe, painless, noninvasive alternative for targeted inch loss. Licensed technicians utilize cold laser technology, in conjunction with whole body vibration, to effectively reduce excess fat from your choice of body part. More than a weight-loss program, Ideal Protein supports cellulite reduction, skin revitalization, improved convalescence, stabilization of blood sugar and other obesity-related conditions.

Southwest

Lynn Fletcher Weddings

403.201.1970
lynnfletcherweddings.com, Twitter: @lynnfletcherwed

Elegant. Comprehensive. Diligent.

With over 15 years' experience in the industry, Lynn and her innovative team produce award-winning weddings that surpass all expectations every time. Exceptional client care and a genuine love for *love* make them the team to call. Lynn has the expertise and creativity to ensure your wedding day perfectly suits you. She has been recognized on teams that have won numerous international awards for "Best Wedding in the World" and takes great pride in never repeating the same wedding style twice. This is *your* day, planned just for you.

Q&A

What tip would you give women who are starting a business?
Look deep inside yourself to see what you are most passionate about. Your heart and spirit have to be in every aspect of the business.

What do you like best about owning a business?
The freedom to do it my way and seeing the results of my team's hard work.

What motivates you on a daily basis?
My clients. We are responsible for the biggest day of their lives!

What is your motto or theme song?
It can't be wrong if it is sparkly!

Lynn Fletcher

Maddpretty Makeover Studio

735 12th Ave SW, Ste 102, Calgary, 403.245.6233
madddpretty.com, Twitter: @BeMaddpretty

Trendy. Artistic. Empowering.
Maddpretty is an education concept makeover studio that delivers serious
skills to teach you the craft of styling whether you work in media or are an
everyday individual looking to pick up some professional instruction; education
is Maddpretty's top priority. It's your one-stop shop for premium makeovers
to reinvent the look that makes you feel like the celebrity that you are.

Photos by Erin Wallace Photography

Jackie Johnson

 Q&A

What are your most popular products or services?
The Deluxe Makeover includes custom cut/colour, hair styling and makeup application with lesson (so you can do the look on your own) and a professional photo of your new look.

What do you like best about owning a business?
Making a difference in one persons self confidence one person at a time.

What motivates you on a daily basis?
Being a "Daymaker" motivates us— it is someone who tries to make a difference—spiritually, emotionally, or financially—in someone's life.

How do you relax?
Mentally separating work from play by embracing the presence of the now.

Teang Tang

Q&A

What tip would you give women who are starting a business?
Focus, focus, *focus*! Be clear on what you are trying to achieve and set aside time to create an action plan on how you will get there.

What motivates you on a daily basis?
The thrill of creating something new every day! When you become inspired, you feel unstoppable—and that rush becomes an addiction for an entrepreneur.

What is your motto or theme song?
"Dynamite" by Taio Cruz.

What do you CRAVE?
That more young women are brave enough to choose entrepreneurship as a viable career choice... because entrepreneurs change the world. The world could use more game changers.

Mingle Event Management Inc.

1611 - 14th St SW, Calgary, 403.561.7849, 604.418.8835
minglemyevent.com, Twitter: @minglemyevent

Chic. Innovative. Fun.
Mingle Event Management Inc. are purveyors of a unique event-planning experience focused on providing eco-luxury event solutions while creating positive change. Mingle services cover corporate, wedding and private events. Mingle was originally founded in Calgary and has grown to include clients in Vancouver and Toronto.

Photos by Kristi Sneddon

Uptown 17th

modern photography

403.680.2360
modernphotography.ca, Twitter: @mod_photo

Genuine. Inspired. Fresh.
Sarah Murdoch is the photography-degree holding, camera-toting, wedding-obsessed pro photographer behind the lens of Calgary-based modern photography. Her natural and calming demeanor affords her the ability to capture the true emotion of her clients. In addition to Sarah's local and international weddings, she also delights in capturing laughter, love and lots of smiles from the families and couples that she photographs.

Q&A

What do you like best about owning a business?
Endless variety and flexibility. I make my own schedule, and I get to make a living doing what I love. I think that is the ultimate dream.

What motivates you on a daily basis?
The fact that my life and success is up to me and no one else.

How do you relax?
Playing soccer, walks with my husband and dog Fenway, coffee or phone dates with friends.

What do you CRAVE?
Amazing light: the kind of glowy, dreamy light that fills in the sky and all the shadows about an hour before sunset. Watch for it. It's magical.

Sarah Murdoch

Angela May

Q&A

What are your most popular products or services?
Money Goddess Mastermind, a 12-month business mentorship program for rapid business and personal growth. Angela May's Business Mastery Academy for Goddesses—a six-figure income level is required to apply.

What tip would you give women who are starting a business?
Always, always have a mentor. Find the right mentor or coach for you and commit yourself to always have one, no matter what.

What do you like best about owning a business?
When I receive a testimonial from a client who has experienced success, I glow for days.

Who is your role model or mentor?
My first mentor was Kendall Summerhawk. I don't know where I would be if I hadn't invested in myself through her.

What is your motto or theme song?
Tell the truth and tell it faster.

What place inspires you and why?
Arizona—a place of incredible energy and transformation.

Money Goddess

moneygoddess.net, Twitter: @missangelamaya

Transformational. Divine. Alchemical.
Money Goddess features live and virtual educational events for women who want to unblock the flow of money into their lives. Courses include structured mastermind programs, marketing secrets courses, monthly workshops. Programs are all based on practical principles, blended with heart and spirit, which often bring the participants massive results—like large increases in income, incredible confidence and a complete reweaving of their personalities.

Q&A

What are your most popular products or services?
Marketing workshops and personal marketing sessions use discussions and doodles to drive decision making. Fans say fun and friendly focused chats, low-tech flip charts and marketing maps inspire big actions and inspiration.

What tip would you give women who are starting a business?
Don't let your business just be a labour of love. Create a plan for profit, too. Success starts with a professional online presence in tandem with a great sales strategy.

What do you like best about owning a business?
It is me at my best! When I've inspired and helped small-business owners as well as my three daughters, I have had a perfect day.

Kim Page Gluckie

MPowered Marketing

403.479.9669, mpoweredmarketing.com, Twitter: @kimpagegluckie

International Alliance of Motivated Part-Time Entrepreneurs

403.479.9669, iampte.com, Twitter: @iampte

Affordable. Effective. Trusted.
Kim is one of the biggest champions, best educators and most generous connectors for small-business owners with big dreams but limited time and money. Kim mentors, motivates and teaches practical, modern marketing concepts through programs, consulting, speeches, workshops and her organization for part-time entrepreneurs. Whether in a class or across a coffee shop table, Kim gives you plans with possibility, focus, clarity and action.

Annie Cole

Q&A

What are your most popular products or services?
Definitely grooming and our jackets from Alco Wasi (100% alpaca and made by fair-trade women's initiatives in Peru... you can't go wrong!) and our organic, fair-trade cleaner made by Cinderella's.

What do you like best about owning a business?
A business has a life of its own that as an owner you can nourish with your personal touches to create something spectacular and better than you ever dreamed!

What motivates you on a daily basis?
The fact that we are able to give dogs a place away from home where they feel safe and that our business choices keep our earth safe as well.

Muttley Crüe Organics

813 1st Ave NE, Calgary, 403.262.6888
muttleycrue.ca

Organic. Sustainable. Positive.
Muttley Crüe is Calgary's first organic, chemical-free and eco-friendly
retail, dog grooming and daycare spa. The concept grew out of a desire to
provide Calgary dog owners with a green, sustainable pet care alternative—
one of only a few in North America. Proud members of REAP Calgary
(reapcalgary.com) and run on 100 percent wind power and love!

Bridgeland

My Sewing Room Inc

148 - 8228 Macleod Trail SE, Calgary, 403.252.3711
mysewingroom.ca, Twitter: @mysewingroomca

Creative. Spectacular. Knowledgeable.

My Sewing Room is Canada's largest independently owned sewing store, featuring more than 15,000 bolts of fabric—including cotton, flannel, batik, wool and other specialty items. My Sewing Room is filled with fabulous eye catching displays of delicious fabrics and an endless selection of notions, patterns and ideas. Learning, teaching and giving back to the community are high priorities for the enthusiastic employees and regular customers.

Anne Dale

Q&A

What are your most popular products or services?
A mountainous selection of quilting and sewing fabrics, notions, sewing machines, classes and the great on-site experienced machine repair people always keep customers coming back.

What tip would you give women who are starting a business?
Decide what you want. Don't take no for an answer, especially from someone not authorized to say yes. Do what you are passionate about and surround yourself with supportive, knowledgeable people.

What place inspires you and why?
I attend several trade conferences a year and the designers, authors and other shop owners who attend inspire me to be more and do more.

Nyla Free Designs

403.862.4980
nylafreedesigns.com, Twitter: @nylafree

Engaging. Confident. Timeless.
Timeless design and detail is offered through Nyla Free Designs, unveiling style and respecting function. Working one-on-one with clients to transform their spaces, Nyla Free bridges classic and unexpected elements to create rooms with presence and panache. Nyla's virtual design packages through Design in a Box is the perfect solution to "get the look" from anywhere.

Q&A

What are your most popular products or services?
Interior design in all aspects from small rooms to large, transitional to modern, one room to entire homes, all customized to each client.

What tip would you give women who are starting a business?
Create a group with like-minded individuals to support, inspire, share ideas and offer advice. Whether social networks or in real life, this camaraderie boosts confidence and encourages in ways unimaginable.

How do you relax?
At the very end of the day, I have a hot bath and catch up on my growing pile of shelter and fashion magazines.

Nyla Free

 Q&A

What tip would you give women who are starting a business?
Surround yourself with good people who enable you to do what you do well. And to know the road ahead, ask those coming back—listening is key.

What do you like best about owning a business?
I love the flexibility it gives me as a mum. I create my schedule around my children's lives and that allows me to always be there for them.

Who is your role model or mentor?
Seventh Generation founder Jeffrey Hollender. The belief that we must look at the impact our actions will have on the next seven generations holds true for our products.

Jane Walter

organicKidz Inc.

403.201.2585
organicKidz.ca, Twitter: @organicKidz

Unique. Innovative. Impacting.
organicKidz™ created the world's first stainless steel baby bottles and first thermal baby bottles to provide children and their parents with the safest, greenest choice. organicKidz bottles are naturally bacteria-resistant, don't shatter like glass or contain the chemicals that plastics can. Best of all, they grow with your child, converting to Sippy Cup and Water Bottle. Better for our children, better for our planet.

Photos by Visual Hues Photography

Pink Spot Studios

403.837.0817
pinkspotstudios.com, Twitter: @PinkSpotStudios

Perceptive. Unconventional. Transformative.
Pink Spot Studios is a boutique art and design company whose primary focus is creating impeccable, one-off design materials for niche brands, locally and internationally. They get to know your business like you do and generate targeted, conceptual and beautiful pieces to connect with your market.

Lia Golemba

Q&A

What are your most popular products or services?
Recently, clients love our large-scale art installations that function as part of their brand. These pieces are dynamic on location and can be re-purposed for print/web materials.

What tip would you give women who are starting a business?
Do what you love... and hire an accountant!

What is your motto or theme song?
Bloom where you are planted.

How do you relax?
I love reading blogs, the minutiae of daily life and the artifacts of people's obsessions are fascinating. Gardening as well, to feel grounded.

Georgina Forrest

 # Q&A

What are your most popular products or services?
Hands-on assistance with organizing both digital and printed photos, providing you with peace of mind. Then turning those photos into meaningful albums to be enjoyed for generations to come.

What tip would you give women who are starting a business?
Build a strong support team. Wisely choose people who you can trust to share your vision, your fears and your doubts. They will be your advocate when you need.

What do you like best about owning a business?
The flexibility to choose and grow my business wherever my passion takes me.

Pix2Pages

403.615.4349, pix2pages.com

Fun. Timeless. Unique.
Too many photos? Too little time? Pix2Pages helps you rediscover your
photos, the stories of your life, and shows you new ways to use them
to connect, share and nurture the important people in your life.

Pretty Little Things

1317 - 9th Ave SE, Calgary, 403.237.5344
prettylittlethings.ca, Twitter: @prettythingsyyc

Stylish. Pretty. Eclectic.
Pretty Little Things is a beautifully curated, new concept boutique featuring an eclectic mix of high-quality, unique treasures.Vintage items, made with craftsmanship and artistry, increasingly rare. From beautiful clothes, shoes, jewellery and accessories to furniture, glassware and books. Quality antiques—pretty as is or more fabulous with a bold coat of paint. Sometimes wild. Sometimes whimsical. Always stylish.

Debbie Dalen

 # Q&A

What are your most popular products or services?
Vintage coats, hats and gloves. Unique lamps, trunks and antique furniture.

What tip would you give women who are starting a business?
Don't let fear hold you back. If you are truly passionate about something, it will guide you in the right direction. Trust yourself and the universe. Your contribution does matter.

What do you like best about owning a business?
I enjoy the freedom I have to do what I feel in my heart is right for my store.

What do you CRAVE?
When I was a young, I thought I had to conform to what everyone else was doing and wearing. Yet, it never felt quite right. I crave people being themselves.

Stephanie Gottlieb and Mae-Lee Khoo

Q&A

What are your most popular products or services?
Our clients most appreciate our ability to present our designs graphically. This allows clients to see our vision for their space and understand precisely how we will transform their interior.

What do you like best about owning a business?
Design is our passion but we work to live, we don't live to work. Privé allows us the flexibility to travel, volunteer and follow our other pursuits as well.

What do you CRAVE?
Travel. Dinner with friends. Wine and cheese. Sitting in the sun. Homemade cakes. Lavish parties. Stilettos. Painting pottery. Indulging in dessert. Primping. Spontaneous shopping sprees. Spanish coffees. LBDs. Interior Design.

Privé Design Group Inc.

403.629.5729, 403.690.8805
privedesigngroup.ca, Twitter: @Steph_Allison, @Miss_Mae_lee

Exclusive. Collaborative. Timeless.

Privé Design Group is a boutique interior design company highly specialized in tailoring each design to the individual. The team's education enables them to offer exceptional design fundamentals paired with a timeless, distinctive style. Their passion for all areas of design is reflected not only through their work, but also in their belief that all aspects of life should emulate beauty, art and functionality.

Photos by Reuben-Lumic Photography, except portrait by Kristi Sneddon

RealTalk

403.278.3077
realtalk-now.com, Twitter: @RealTalk_Now

Heartfelt. Open. Powerful.

RealTalk teaches people to have conversations that build relationships. Through the practice and application of the Great Eight powerful questions and deep listening, people experience closer connections, more trust and respect, stronger influence and wonderfully satisfying relationships with family, friends and colleagues. Using the Three RealTalk Principles of authentic presence, self-direction and full engagement, you can begin to have the kinds of conversations that build the relationships you long for.

Dawnie Heartwell and Tammy Robertson
(Rashmi Malhotra not pictured)

Q&A

What tip would you give women who are starting a business?
People will ask you tough questions. Be ready to talk about what matters most. Always ask yourself the question, "What conversation needs to happen now?"

What do you like best about owning a business?
The opportunity to fully express and contribute in a way that is personally relevant and that is in line with what we are passionate about.

What motivates you on a daily basis?
People who have transformed their lives through a deeper belief in themselves and each other keep us jazzed about what we are doing. Our constant question is how do we help people reconnect with themselves and with each other, so they can have the most amazing love affair with life?

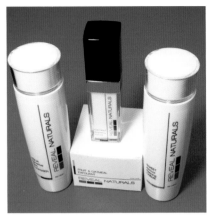

Catherine Bambrough

Q&A

What tip would you give women who are starting a business?
Have a good system... whether that is a computer system or a personal system—just have one that works and that can grow with you.

What do you like best about owning a business?
Working for myself is rewarding. I may sound like a broken record, but I get to meet wonderful people every day, and helping them achieve their goals is an amazing feeling!

What motivates you on a daily basis?
My clients—when they are excited about their results, it motivates me to keep going... to keep helping.

What is your motto or theme song?
Reveal a New You!

Reveal Rejuvenation Inc.

By appointment only: 6036 3rd St SW, Ste 104, Calgary, 403.457.3588
revealrejuv.ca

Life-altering. Inexpensive. Respectful.
Reveal Rejuvenation Inc. offers a variety of noninvasive, nonsurgical cosmetic procedures that help you achieve your goals toward a more youthful, healthy appearance. A customized prescription for rejuvenation can be created based on your goals; then utilizing the best in laser/light technologies and spa therapies, you'll be given the results you're looking for—plus education on preventative factors to avoid further aging and damage.

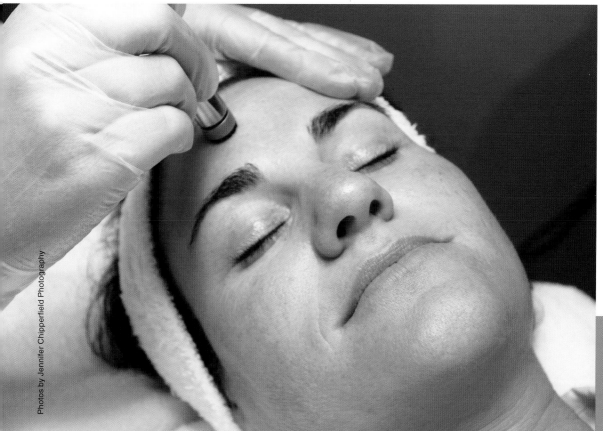

Photos by Jennifer Chipperfield Photography

Southwest

Rewind
Consignment Clothing

1002 Macleod Trail SE, Calgary, 403.263.6669
rewindconsignment.com, Twitter: @RewindClothing

Stylish. Charming. Organized.

Despite the name, Rewind is a fashion-forward boutique offering new and resale clothing and accessories in an inviting atmosphere. You will find designer labels as well as popular brands and unique one-of-a-kind items adorning the racks and shelves in this unique heritage space. Enjoy a friendly shopping experience with staff that love fashion and handpick merchandise just for you!

Krista Hopfauf

Q&A

What are your most popular products or services?
Unique, independently designed jewellery and accessories (many local); selective, hand-picked resale clothing from popular to more obscure brands, and high-end designer pieces; unique boutique brands; personal shopping/styling; private shopping parties.

What tip would you give women who are starting a business?
Make sure it's something you're passionate about and believe in. If you do something you love, everything else will fall into place. Don't let fear hold you back.

What is your motto or theme song?
Life isn't about finding yourself; it's about creating yourself.

"The Fire Within" Acupuncture and Wellness
photographed by modern photography

What is your motto or theme song?

"*What lies behind us and what lies before us are tiny matters compared to what lies within us.*" —*Ralph Waldo Emerson. This powerful quote speaks volumes for Spiritual empowerment.*

Dr. Tanya Hartz of "The Fire Within" Acupuncture and Wellness

Cat Hackman

 # Q&A

What are your most popular products or services?
Furniture, art and accessories sourcing/placement and colour consultations. I also do floor plans and 3-D renderings as well as small renovations including selecting hard surfaces, flooring, tile, plumbing fixtures, lighting, etc.

What do you like best about owning a business?
Flexibility in balancing my time between family and work. Being accountable for my own success.

What is your motto or theme song?
Life's too short to not surround yourself with beauty! Positive thoughts = a positive life.

What do you CRAVE?
Happiness and health for my family, friends and for myself. And a bit of salty liquorice.

Room4Refinement

403.681.4473
room4refinement.com, Twitter: @Roomrefiner

Functional. Inspirational. Approachable.
Cat Hackman strives to make your home stylish, comfortable and practical, and all within a reasonable budget. During a refinement consultation, Cat will work with you as a team, and in the process, you'll learn to correct the most common decorating mistakes. Cat will also create floor plans and help you choose colours, furniture, lighting, flooring, area rugs, tile, countertops, window treatments, accessories and more.

Photos by Bien Chic, except portrait by Kristi Sneddon

Sagebrook Developments Inc.

403.453.0090, sagebrook.ca, Twitter: @SagebrookHomes

Innovative. Urban-chic. Reliable.
Buying or building an inner-city home is not just about the home, it's a lifestyle. At Sagebrook Developments, their custom inner-city infills are not only built with quality but with the urban professional lifestyle in mind. Sagebrook is family-owned and -operated and is proud to offer the "family treatment" in customer service and quality products.

Q&A

What tip would you give women who are starting a business?
Always take risks: it's how you learn and it makes you stronger. "If you risk nothing, then you risk everything." —Geena Davis

What do you like best about owning a business?
The flexibility, working with my family and seeing my vision come to life.

Who is your role model or mentor?
My father. He encouraged me to work hard and not let barriers of being a minority get in the way of my dreams.

What place inspires you and why?
Completed projects. Seeing my vision come to life and knowing that it has made other people happy.

Kristine Yung

Sam Rafoss

Q&A

What are your most popular products or services?
Complimentary Q&A call. Many entrepreneurs don't know where to start. I openly and honestly discuss how I can best help or offer tips based on their current status.

What tip would you give women who are starting a business?
Believe in yourself and love what you do. Trust your gut instincts always. Write down your plan and goals. Focus on your strengths and ask for help with the rest.

What do you like best about owning a business?
Doing what I love—teaching, mentoring and inspiring other women entrepreneurs to achieve their dreams while creating my schedule to be around for my kids. You can't beat that.

What motivates you on a daily basis?
My three amazing daughters. They are my cherished gifts. I'm honoured to be their mom and strive to live what I wish for them—love, laughter, health, happiness, success.

What is your motto or theme song?
Never ever give up, and look for the good in everyone and everything.

Sam Rafoss

403.988.7507
samrafoss.com, Twitter: @SamRafoss

Inspiring. Empowering. Intuitive.
Sam Rafoss is a business consultant, coach, mentor, workshop leader and speaker
who passionately educates and empowers female entrepreneurs in the health
and wellness field to achieve their goals so they can have the life of their dreams.
Her mission and commitment is to show women how to believe in themselves and
confidently help their clients best by attaining the success and prosperity they desire.

Photos by Kristi Sneddon

Q&A

What are your most popular products or services?
Our hand-mixed spice blends are always favourites with our customers. From barbeque rubs to curry powders, Herbes de Provence to Za'atar Seasoning, you will find just what you need.

What is your biggest fear?
My biggest fear is behind me—it was that I would have a great idea for a business but wouldn't have the guts to go for it.

What motivates you on a daily basis?
The knowledge that I can always make my business even better. There is so much room to grow and improve that I don't think I could ever get bored.

Kelci Hind

The Silk Road Spice Merchant

1403A - 9th Ave SE, Calgary, 403.261.1955
silkroadspices.ca, Twitter: @silkroadspices

Inviting. Exotic. Immersive.
The Silk Road offers a complete range of spices, herbs, chiles and seasonings from around the world. They take great care to source the finest products available, and the spices are the freshest you'll find anywhere. All spice blends are hand-mixed and have been developed and perfected in-house. The Silk Road is located in Inglewood and also has a stall in the Calgary Farmers' Market.

Skintelligence Ltd.

2032 34th Ave SW, Calgary, 403.229.9474
skintelligence.ca

Friendly. Pampering. Attentive.

Skintelligence Beauty Salon is celebrating 25 years of pampering loyal clients, while welcoming new faces with equal enthusiasm. Tina and her team are passionate about achieving radiance and rejuvenating every guest on the inside and out. They offer effective treatments that give your skin a gorgeous youthful glow as well as manicures, pedicures, waxing and massages that will refresh your mind, body and soul.

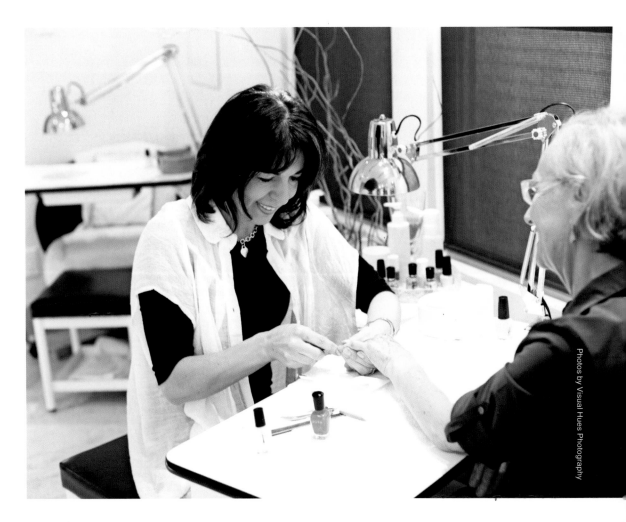

Photos by Visual Hues Photography

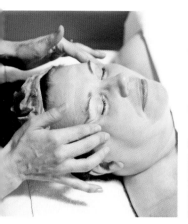

ENJOY   RELAX

Tina Bilt

Q&A

What are your most popular
products or services?
European facials, manicures and pedicures,
skincare from Laboratoire Dr. Renaud.

What do you like best about
owning a business?
I love being able to pamper
clients in my own way.

What motivates you on a daily basis?
My fabulous clients. Happy clients
make me happy.

How do you relax?
Spending time with my family.

What place inspires you and why?
Europe; specifically, the different cultures,
fashion and the overall uniqueness.

Michele Beitel

Q&A

What tip would you give women
who are starting a business?
Write a comprehensive business
plan, get honest feedback from other
successful entrepreneurs, then rewrite
your plan! Be open to evolution.

How do you relax?
With a glass of wine, good friends and great
conversation, the hours seem like minutes.

What place inspires you and why?
New York: the city has energy
24 hours a day, is leading-edge
and has an entrepreneurial core.
You can make anything and
everything happen in New York.

The Skoop

403.850.8485
theskoop.ca, Twitter: @gettheskoop

Exclusive. Effortless. Connected.
The Skoop is an exclusive social lifestyle club that keeps members connected
with the best events, adventures and activities in the city. The Skoop aids in
marketing efforts by raising the awareness and quality of events and the companies
hosting those events. The Skoop does this by sending members invites based
on their preferences, thus being able to directly target the right audience.

Photos by SDS Creative and Inspire Studios, except portrait
by Jennifer Chipperfield Photography

 Q&A

What are your most popular
products or services?
Giftware, home decor, ladies
accessories, toys, greeting cards,
personalized stationery and invitations

What tip would you give women
who are starting a business?
Don't do it alone. Make sure you
have a great support system.

What is your motto or theme song?
When you have exhausted all possibilities,
remember this: you haven't.

How do you relax?
By visiting the wine store next
door for wine tastings.

Dawn Messer and Kathie James

The Social Page

839 - 10th Ave SW, Calgary, 403.245.8868
thesocialpage.ca, Twitter: @thesocialpage

Creative. Eclectic. Fun.
The Social Page continues to be the place to go for creative and
unique invitations. After 19 years in business, they have expanded
their product range to become a premiere giftware store!

Sol Swimwear

403.519.7232
solswimwear.com, Twitter: @solswimwear

Comfortable. Flattering. Honest.
Sol Swimwear specializes in helping women find the most flattering, unique and beautiful swimwear for their body types. Whether clients prefer one-on-one appointments in the privacy of Sol's intimate boutique, the comfort of a consultation in their own home or a "Girl's Night Out" Swimwear Party, Sol Swimwear works with women of all shapes and sizes to build confidence while wearing swimwear.

 # Q&A

Tricia Andres McDonald

What are your most popular products or services?
One-on-one appointments in the Sol Swimwear Boutique offer an intimate and honest swimwear shopping experience. Clients love the uniqueness of the collections offered from around the world.

What motivates you on a daily basis?
Seeing my clients smile while wearing a bathing suit, I know that they will rock it on the beach. Women with confidence can rule the world!

What place inspires you and why?
Rio de Janeiro inspires me, not only because the vibe throughout the city is so relaxed but because of the entrepreneurial spirit of the people there.

Sophie Klassen
Urban Living Calgary

403.863.7235
urbanlivingcalgary.ca, Twitter: @sophieklassen

Sincere. Involved. Rewarding.

Ever since she was a young girl, Sophie wanted to own her own business; her passion and love for meeting, helping and educating people brought her to real estate. Sophie's personalized, honest, refreshing approach to buying and selling real estate is what sets her apart. As an agent for Century 21 Bamber Realty Ltd., Sophie is here to assist in your lifestyle evolution by listening to your needs, adding her knowledge and expertise.

Sophie Klassen

Q&A

What are your most popular products or services?
Assisting clients in buying and selling real estate. I will be your personal advocate, expert strategist and skilled negotiator.

What motivates you on a daily basis?
Seeing the sparkle in my clients' eyes when they take possession of their new home, knowing they're thinking about the new life chapter that is about to begin!

What is your motto or theme song?
"Live with intention. Listen hard. Practice wellness. Laugh. Choose with no regret. Appreciate your friends. Continue to learn. Do what you love. Live as if this is all there is." —Mary Anne Radmacher

Soul Reflection

403.990.0123
soulreflection.ca, Twitter: @reflectyoursoul

Empowering. Engaging. Unexpected.
Soul Reflection is a personal styling and image coaching company led by Kelli Harker. Kelli focuses on empowering women through image and believes that any woman can look her best regardless of age or weight. Kelli is an expert in where to shop in Calgary and specializes in petite and plus sizing.

Kelli Harker

Q&A

What are your most popular products or services?
Closet audits, custom-look books, personal shopping, facilitated shopping trips to NYC, personal color analysis, "fashion FUNdamentals" home parties and seminars.

What motivates you on a daily basis?
When I witness a woman's face light up as she sees herself in an outfit she never would have picked on her own.

What is your motto or theme song?
Your image says something. So mean what it says.

What place inspires you and why?
New York City feels like my second home. The energy fuels me, and I feel alive when I am there regardless if it is for business or pleasure.

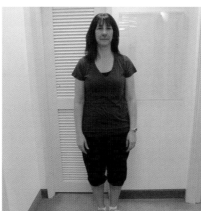

Stephanie Pollock

Q&A

What are your most popular products or services?
The Activator Sessions: A 30-day full-immersion, brand-building intensive designed for the entrepreneur ready to blaze new trails, step up into their full leadership potential and make some serious profit.

What tip would you give women who are starting a business?
Figure out early what you believe in. Bold, brilliant brands aren't afraid to take a stand. Trying to accommodate everyone is a sure way to blend in.

What do you like best about owning a business?
Freedom. I started my business because I wanted freedom to pursue my wild and crazy ideas, be home with my kids and to create an awesome life on my terms.

What motivates you on a daily basis?
My kids and clients. My kids remind me to live fully and in the moment, and my clients remind me that anything is possible when you do what you love.

What is your motto or theme song?
"It's never too late to be what you might have become." —George Eliot

Stephanie Pollock Media Inc.

403.988.7708
stephaniepollock.com, Twitter: @steph_pollock

Bold. Sassy. Game-changing.
As Brand Activator + Coach for Stephanie Pollock Media Inc., Stephanie is on a mission to help women entrepreneurs brand their brilliance and ignite their income. Stephanie has a unique gift for uncovering the genius deep inside her clients through her signature Activate Brand YOU process. She inspires women to identify their brand's brilliance factor and position it powerfully for maximum impact and income.

SweptAway
Green Cleaning

403.605.8101
sweptawaygreen.com, Twitter: @SweptAwayGreen

Eco-friendly. Fabulous. Guaranteed.
Exceptional, efficient and eco-friendly are just some of the words used to describe SweptAway! They are a highly recommended premiere residential/commercial cleaning company using only eco-friendly cleaning products. While they are a fast growing, independently owned company, they haven't deviated from a strong work ethic and still insist on providing a personal touch. It's their nature, it's their business and it's your reward!

Dulcee Stoodley

Q&A

What are your most popular products or services?
Clients love that we are committed to the well-being of the environment—and it won't cost the Earth! Many find our detailed bi-weekly service perfect for their needs.

What tip would you give women who are starting a business?
You will be successful when you follow through with your vision, with passion, smarts, hard work and a belief that anything is possible!

What do you like best about owning a business?
The energy and feedback that I get from clients and acquaintances regarding SweptAway's meticulous teamwork and our "green cleaning" concept.

What motivates you on a daily basis?
The energy from clients who are so thankful to our teams for giving them some peace of mind in a beautifully clean space to reside!

How do you relax?
Meditation and exercise every day.

What do you CRAVE?
Educating and promoting green cleaning services for a healthy, productive and environmentally responsible atmosphere in which to live and work!

Tara Whittaker

Q&A

What tip would you give women
who are starting a business?
Do your research, believe in yourself and
finally, be patient. Building a successful
business takes time and effort.

Who is your role model or mentor?
My mother is an inspiring model of
independence, determination and hard
work. She has tried many new things in her
life, always with a focus on serving others.

What is your biggest fear?
Mediocrity.

What motivates you on a daily basis?
I view photography as a gift to be used and
a craft to be honed. I'm constantly looking
for ways to improve my client's experience.

Tara Whittaker Photography

403.247.3746
tarawhittaker.com, Twitter: @tarawhitphoto

Playful. Pretty. Passionate.

Tara's work is rooted in fine art photography and has appeared in galleries around Alberta. Tara approaches wedding photography from the viewpoint of a storyteller, capturing each wedding through a unique blend of photojournalism, creative posing and fine art photography. Says Whittaker, "Weddings have it all—beauty, drama, expectation, detail, pure joy, silliness and raw emotion. They are thrilling to be a part of."

Photos by Tara Whittaker Photography, except portrait by Tara Whitney

Fay Ostafichuk

Q&A

What tip would you give women who are starting a business?
Passion and commitment. If you have these working for you, the many challenges and obstacles that will surely come your way will be easily and creatively managed.

What do you like best about owning a business?
Having the freedom to live my dream of providing a unique combination of services and products that helps our clients to realize their true inner and outer beauty.

What motivates you on a daily basis?
My purpose: providing a beautiful space for uplifting our clients' spirits.

What is your motto or theme song?
Where inner peace and outer beauty meet.

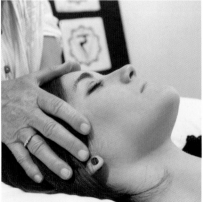

Photos by Kristi Sneddon

ThairAPY Serenity and Beauty Services

1881 85 St NW, Calgary, 403.247.6440
thairapy.ca

Unique. Inviting. Relaxing.
Located conveniently in the hip community of Montgomery, Thairapy Serenity and Beauty Services have created an environment for the realization of true personal beauty through their unique combined skills of talented hairstylists, energy practitioners and aestheticians. Using eco-friendly products wherever possible, Thairapy provides a healthy, reflective atmosphere for both clients and staff.

The Think Sun Preschool Academy

By appointment only: 10 - 5555 Strathcona Hill SW, Calgary, 403.240.4466
thethinksunpreschool.com

Unique. Creative. Nurturing.
The Think Sun Preschool, currently in its 22nd successful year of operation, prepares preschoolers for a kindergarten classroom. Their unique and creative fine arts activities and program are specifically designed to engage preschoolers at an age-appropriate level.

Maureen Khallad

Q&A

What are your most popular
products or services?
We offer two levels of programs.
The first level is for 3-year-olds and
the Junior Kindergarten second
level is for 4- and 5-year-olds.

What tip would you give women
who are starting a business?
Starting a business is a leap of faith. Listen
to your intuition. Believe in your product.
Start small. Ensure that your business is
always top-notch. Treat your staff well.

What do you like best about
owning a business?
I love teaching preschoolers and have
a passion for preschool education.
I further enjoy the challenge of
growing my own business.

Southwest

Shashi Behl

Q&A

What do you like best about owning a business?
I love learning and being challenged. It is totally inspiring to see an idea come to fruition and constantly change the way you think. I also love owning my time.

Who is your role model or mentor?
My role model would be my dad. He taught me how to work hard and prioritize my time. His favorite saying is "the harder you work, the luckier you get."

What place inspires you and why?
Thailand. The people who live there are warm and kind and know that you can't settle anything by raising your voice and arguing. It also has great weather and beaches.

Twisted Goods

Market Mall, Calgary, 403.247.6691
South Centre Mall, Calgary, 403.452.6086
Aspen Landing Shopping Centre, Calgary, 403.453.0109
twistedgoods.ca, Twitter: @TwistedGoods

Unique. Eclectic. Warm.

Twisted Goods is a store that moves with the latest trends and is constantly evolving. If you are looking for a funky, unique conversation piece to show your personality and bring a modern vibe to your space or you just need something fun to brighten a friend's day, you will find it at Twisted Goods. Twisted Goods is nothing you need and everything you want!

Gloria Christie

Q&A

What do you like best about owning a business?
I enjoy wowing women one tour at a time! Enriching women's lives with unforgettable travel experiences is the best part of owning my own business.

Who is your role model or mentor?
Bruce Poon Tip—visionary leader of G Adventures. A big-picture thinker who believes in extraordinary experiences. He's a smart man with a conscience.

What motivates you on a daily basis?
Retirement. Knowing that one day I'll have more time to devote to having fun!

What place inspires you and why?
Greece. It reminds me that simple is beautiful and that family is the foundation lives are built upon.

Ultimate Chicktrips

403.837.8405
ultimatechicktrips.com, Twitter: @glo_chicktrips

Fun. Fabulous. Unforgettable.
Lead by Facilitator of Fun, Gloria Christie, Ultimate Chicktrips is known for its big-fun, small-group, unique escorted tours to fabulous places. Incorporating the best of what each destination has to offer into the custom-designed itineraries is key for Ultimate Chicktrips. Believe it when women say an Ultimate Chicktrips tour is more than just a trip because it truly is an unforgettable experience!

Urban Venus Nail Bar

#113, 638 - 11th Ave SW, Calgary, 403.266.1158
#3001, 873 - 85th St SW, Calgary, 403.686.0997
urbanvenus.ca, Twitter: @urbanvenus

Cosmopolitan. Indulgent. Trendsetting.
Urban Venus is a modern and fresh nail bar where you can drop in for a service
or make a party booking for a posh private event. Urban Venus makes its own
line of products and has been featured in national magazines as one of the top
spots in the country to get manicured. UV has polished the nails of Lady Gaga,
Katy Perry, Miley Cyrus, the Black Eyed Peas and many other celebrities.

Photos by modern photography, except main photo

Rachel Ong

Q&A

What are your most popular products or services?
Our custom nail polish, delicious lotions and our fresh-squeezed pedicure are favourites among our clientele.

What tip would you give women who are starting a business?
Follow your instincts, surround yourself with positive people, don't take yourself too seriously and give back to the community that supports you.

What do you like best about owning a business?
I am able to meet many creative people who are inspirational industry leaders.

What place inspires you and why?
SoHo, in New York City, because it has a high level of enthusiasm, creativity and originality all in one concentrated area.

Vision 2000 Travel

403.455.1161
tanjawalsh.com, Twitter: @tanjawalsh

Niche. Reliable. Collaborative.
Tanja Walsh is an independent luxury travel advisor for Vision 2000, Canada's leading Virtuoso agency. She expertly plans and designs destination weddings and honeymoons worldwide. Whether you are planning a vacation for two or 200, if you are budget-minded or luxury-minded, your vacation will be as you have envisioned it because of her industry experience and insider connections.

Tanja Walsh

 # Q&A

What are your most popular products or services?
Destination wedding and honeymoon planning are the most popular services. From there, I am booking their cruises, family adventures and trips of a lifetime. I grow with my clients!

What tip would you give women who are starting a business?
I believe you cannot be a part-time entrepreneur; you have to give it all you got. Be very passionate and knowledgeable about your product or service.

What is your motto or theme song?
"Go the extra mile. It is never crowded." —Anonymous

Janet Pliszka

Q&A

What tip would you give women who are starting a business?
Keep true to yourself, nurture mutually beneficial relationships with other businesses, establish systems and processes from the beginning and hire experts where needed.

What do you like best about owning a business?
I know its my decisions, passion and dedication that contribute to the huge pride I feel when I walk through the doors of my studio.

What motivates you on a daily basis?
Connection. Connection with my family and my friends. Connection with my clients. Connection is what builds trust, love, joy and happiness. It also is the foundation for timeless images.

Visual Hues Photography Inc.

By appointment only: 2024 - 34th Ave SW, Calgary, 403.252.7971
visualhues.com, Twitter: @janetpliszka

Trusted. Warm. Genuine.
Visual Hues Photography Studio and Garden focuses on capturing authentic moments and connections between families. Their photographers provide timeless photography inside the cozy studio, outside in the landscaped backyard, in clients' homes and beautiful outdoor locations. Clients can expect a holistic experience from the moment of booking to their shoot to their ordering session, with photos that last generations.

Vital Benefits Inc.

403.209.3817
vitalbenefitsinc.com, Twitter: @vitalbenefits

Innovative. Collaborative. Caring.
Vital Benefits is an employee benefits and individual insurance consulting firm that offers top-tier service to clients. Organizations value the "high touch" service model and innovation that they bring to both small and mid-sized companies.

Andrea Shandro, Laura Barkley,
Melanie Jeannotte and Jennifer Kirby

Q&A

What tip would you give women
who are starting a business?
Follow your marketing plan. Be
consistent and give it time to work;
the only thing that you can control
is your own activity. Specialize and
develop processes for everything.

What do you like best about
owning a business?
Creating a team and work environment
with a values-based approach to doing
business—and having flexibility.

What motivates you on a daily basis?
We really do help people! When health
events occur or we resolve claims issues,
we know we've made a difference.

What is your motto?
Work to your expertise, focus on
your strengths.

What place inspires you and why?
Calgary! This city has a tremendous amount
of energy and appetite for entrepreneurship.

What do you CRAVE?
Constant challenges, the success of all
the fantastic people who have helped
make us what we are, and the elusive
balance between work and family life.

The Willows Spa

230 - 412 Pine Creek Rd, DeWinton, 403.257.9623
thewillowsspa.com, Twitter: @thewillowsspa

Professional. Rejuvenating. Comforting.

The Willows Spa has a very comforting environment from the moment you step in. From their country location to their friendly staff, they look forward to seeing you, each and every visit, and will make you feel welcome. The professional staff at the Willows care about your personal needs and want to provide you with the best service possible!

Photos by Jennifer Chipperfield Photography

Kathryn Chong

Q&A

What are your most popular
products or services?
Our Willows Signature Facial, Dermalogica's
Age Smart Facial, Therapeutic Pedicure and
any type of Massage Therapy: deep tissue,
relaxation, hot stone and Swedish massage.

What tip would you give women
who are starting a business?
Remember to look up from the task
at hand and take that bird's-eye look
at your business. It's a completely
different perspective!

What do you like best about
owning a business?
I love to learn. Owning a business provides
me with ongoing learning, and I love
the personal rewards of hard work.

DeWinton

Lori Danyluk

 # Q&A

What are your most popular products or services?
Our evening gatherings are a wonderful blend of people, creativity, yummy food and wine or tea. Inspiring projects and interesting women are a great combination for a fabulous evening out.

What motivates you on a daily basis?
The peace and joy that I see on the faces of the women who attend our workshops never fail to remind me of what a privilege this "work" is.

What is your motto or theme song?
"When I dare to be powerful—to use my strength in the service of my vision, then it becomes less and less important whether I am afraid." —Audre Lorde

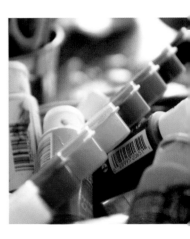

Wine, Women and a Paintbrush

403.975.5978
winewomenandapaintbrush.com

Thought-provoking. Creative. Renewing.
A creative, fun, 3-hour escape from your busy daily lives, Wine, Women and a Paintbrush provides everything you need: supplies, wine and tea, nibbles, music... Different monthly art projects are designed to inspire you and remind you who you are when you're not buried under everything else. Gain insights or take a needed break. You don't need to be artistic, just enthusiastic!

Q&A

What are your most popular products or services?
Office de-cluttering, file system setup and computer-competency training to save you hours per week. Guidance to select the best free and low-cost technology solutions for your business.

What tip would you give women who are starting a business?
Quick and consistent response time—always respond within 24 hours to all inquiries. Being first to respond has ensured I beat out my competition on countless occasions.

What do you like best about owning a business?
Meeting other amazing businesswomen and making inspiring and energizing connections!

Who is your role model or mentor?
Julie Morgenstern, author of *Organizing from the Inside Out*, who inspired me to start my business in 2002. I recently met her, and she continues to motivate me!

What is your motto or theme song?
Keep it simple—organizing is not rocket science! It's about developing simple systems and adapting them as needed.

Dawn O'Connor

Work in Order

403.455.0228
workinorder.com, Twitter: @workinorder

Passionate. Pragmatic. Professional.
It all starts with your source of mess or stress. Work in Order's Productivity
Professionals deliver practical desk-side training focused on your ergonomic
comfort, technology, habits and work flow. Tailored solutions help you beat
stress, save time, increase profitability and feel more in control of your work.
Do you want to love your office and feel inspired to do your best work?

Photos by Visual Hues Photography

Your Friendly Bookkeeper

403.616.1352
yourfriendlybookkeeper.ca, Twitter: @yfbookkeeper

Empowering. Fun. Approachable.
Your Friendly Bookkeeper (YFB) provides dedicated, professional service for business owners looking to experience freedom from cumbersome bookkeeping and administrative worries to run their businesses and serve their clients. YFB believes the day-to-day tasks of keeping a business running and successful can be fun and friendly—those probably weren't the first "f" words that came to mind when you thought of bookkeeping, were they?

Photos by Tara Whittaker Photography

⬛ Q&A

What are your most popular products or services?
Our customized annual bookkeeping packages are the most popular. Secondly, payroll support, which provides assistance to owners paying their employees. And newly popular, administration services, outsourcing to keep costs down.

What tip would you give women who are starting a business?
There's a lot of free advice out there; don't take advice from someone who's not at least as successful as you. Follow your intuition; it will lead you perfectly.

What do you like best about owning a business?
Helping others succeed in their business, giving them the support they need right when they need it.

What motivates you on a daily basis?
Empowering women! Both by supporting them in their businesses and hiring Associates to be a part of Your Friendly Bookkeeper.

What is your motto or theme song?
Live. Love. Laugh. We could all use a little more of each in our lives everyday.

Debbi Chapman

Katherine Kinch

Q&A

What tip would you give women
who are starting a business?
When you truly care about your
clients and the service you provide,
your business will blossom.

What do you like best about
owning a business?
Working hard to grow something I
can be proud of and call my own.

Who is your role model or mentor?
My mom who gave me the gardening
bug and an appreciation for color that
has evolved into a passion for creating
beautiful spaces for people to enjoy.

What motivates you on a daily basis?
Knowing that each new client brings a
project that is unique and inspiring.

Your Space By Design

403.971.5363, katherine@yourspacebydesign.com
YourSpaceByDesign.com

Inspired. Personalized. Functional.
Your Space By Design provides design services for interior and exterior living spaces. They create environments that are an expression of their clients' personality and style while maintaining functionality. Specializing in landscape design, they plan the outdoor space to be an extension of the indoor, incorporating outdoor rooms that encourage you to stop and stay awhile.

Index

By Category

By Category (continued)

By Neighborhood

Contributors

We believe in acknowledging, celebrating and passionately supporting locally owned businesses and entrepreneurs. We are extremely grateful to all contributors for this publication.

CRAVE Founder

thecravecompany.com
startupjunkie.com

MELODY BIRINGER

Innovative. Feminine. Connective.

Melody Biringer, self-avowed "start-up junkie," has built companies that range from Biringer Farm, a family-run specialty-food business, to home furnishings to a fitness studio.

Her current entrepreneurial love-child is The CRAVE Company, a network of businesses designed to creatively connect entrepreneurs who approach business in a fresh new way with the stylish consumers they desire. The CRAVE family includes CRAVEparty, CRAVEguides and CRAVEbusiness. What started out as girlfriends getting together for exclusive glam-gal gatherings, CRAVEparty has since expanded into CRAVEbusiness, a resource for entrepreneurs seeking a modern approach, and CRAVEguides, delivering style and substance. Since initially launching in Seattle, Melody has taken CRAVE to more than 30 cities worldwide, including New York City, Boston, Los Angeles, Chicago, Amsterdam and Toronto.

Melody is a loyal community supporter, versed traveler and strong advocate for women-owned businesses.

CRAVE Calgary Partner

403.971.4555, kconsulting.ca
Twitter: @kconsulting

WENDY KENNELLY

Compassionate. Modest. Creative.
Wendy Kennelly is an entrepreneurial, self-motivated professional who loves a challenge!

She is a patient listener who can quickly assess business roadblocks (present and future) and map out creative solutions to increase productivity and profitability.

Her background is diverse and colorful. Beyond creating a national field marketing and events agency in 1999, Wendy has had the privilege of playing a leading role in many organizations. Aside from being a busy mom, wife and entrepreneur, Wendy is an active community volunteer.

CRAVE Calgary Partner

403.923.0641, caley@craveparty.com
Twitter: @caleyremington

CALEY REMINGTON

Outgoing. Spirited. Thoughtful.
After using her communications degree as a launching pad for a career in media and entertainment, Caley Remington has been able to wear many hats within the industry. As a reporter, producer, consultant and writer, Caley had the opportunity to explore the world, but the western spirit drew her back to the mountains. She is thrilled to be starting her family and consulting company in Calgary.

With CRAVE Calgary, she was excited to rediscover the gems of Calgary and showcase the fabulous gifts the women in the CRAVE community have to offer.

Contributors (continued)

Alison Turner
graphic designer
alisonjturner.com

Alison is a passionate designer and critical thinker from Seattle. She supports human rights and the local food movement. She enjoys researching interesting things, volunteering, being outside, dancing, cooking and running.

Amanda Buzard
lead designer
amandabuzard.com

Amanda is a Seattle native inspired by clean patterns and vintage design. She chases many creative and active pursuits in her spare time, including photography, baking, attempting DIY projects and exploring the beautiful Pacific Northwest.

Lilla Kovacs
operations manager
lilla@thecravecompany.com

As the operations manager, Lilla ensures that everything runs like clockwork. In her limited spare time, she enjoys baking, shoe shopping, traveling, art, Apple products and daydreaming about her hometowns, Arad, Romania and Tel-Aviv, Israel.

Mollie Ruiz-Hopper
social media director
mollie@thecravecompany.com
mollieinseattle.com

A Seattle native, Mollie enjoys nothing more than walking through downtown in high heels with a latte in one hand and her cell phone in the other. She is inspired by CRAVE and is slightly obsessed with social media.

Nicole Shema
project manager
nicole@thecravecompany.com

A Seattle native, Nicole is happy to be back in her city after graduating from the University of Oregon in 2009. Nicole has a passion for travel, and she loves discovering new places around Seattle with friends, running, shopping, and reading in coffee shops.

Carrie Wicks
copy editor
linkedin.com/in/carriewicks

Carrie has been proofreading professionally for 14-plus years in mostly creative fields. When she's not proofreading or copyediting, she's reading, singing jazz, walking in the woods or gardening.

Craving Savings

Get the savings you crave with the following participating businesses—one time only!

- [ ] **Aim4fitness**
  20% off your first personal training session

- [ ] **Aliki's Art House / Art in Mind**
  complimentary 2nd session of Art as Therapy

- [ ] **Anne Wright Photography**
  10% off product order for a lifestyle/family shoot

- [ ] **Apex Massage Therapy / Spagoes**
  $20 off a one-hour massage

- [ ] **Artists Within Makeup Academy**
  40% off pro makeup line

- [ ] **Beauty Uncovered**
  25% discount

- [ ] **breathe hot yoga**
  $25 off a one-month unlimited membership

- [ ] **Compassionate Beauty**
  20% discount

- [ ] **The Creative Tree Early Learning Centre Inc.**
  15% discount

- [ ] **Dance Through Life**
  5 Zumba or Zumba Toning Classes for $40

- [ ] **doo-dads**
  10% discount

- [ ] **Elford Communications**
  free 1-hour communications consulting session

- [ ] **The Ferocious Grape**
  15% discount

- [ ] **"The Fire Within" Acupuncture and Wellness**
  25% off shamanic workshop

- [ ] **First Step Nutrition**
  10% off a nutrition package

- [ ] **Flora**
  15% discount

- [ ] **Fresh Cleanse**
  $50 discount

- [ ] **Fresh Start Yoga**
  50% off 10 classes in a registered session

- [ ] **Gemma Stone International Inc.**
  free workshop and 50% off one-on-one

- [ ] **gravity kidz**
  20% discount (not to be combined with any other offer)

- [ ] **Haute Tots**
  15% discount

- [ ] **Jennifer Chipperfield**
  10% discount

- [ ] **Jennifer Powter**
  20% discount

- [ ] **Kathryn Aston Interiors**
  30% off of manufacturer's suggested retail price

- [ ] **Lauren Lane Decor**
  $25 off beginners class

- [ ] **Lavender Breeze The Lavender Shoppe**
  $5.00 discount

- [ ] **Lipolaser Solutions**
  25% discount

- [ ] **Lynn Fletcher Weddings**
  free gift when you book a consultation

- [ ] **Maddpretty Makeover Studio**
  35% off a salon service

- [ ] **Mingle Event Management Inc.**
  25% off event services

- [ ] **modern photography**
  receive one additional hour of wedding photography

Craving Savings

☐ **Money Goddess**
$20 off a live local event

☐ **MPowered Marketing /
International Alliance of Motivated
Part-Time Entrepreneurs**
*free 20-minute GET FOCUSED
FAST marketing consult*

☐ **Muttley Crüe Organics**
20% off any first-time grooming service

☐ **My Sewing Room Inc**
10% discount

☐ **Pink Spot Studios**
10% discount

☐ **Pix2Pages**
15% off of first package

☐ **Reveal Rejuvenation Inc.**
10% discount

☐ **Rewind Consignment Clothing**
10% discount

☐ **Sagebrook Developments Inc.**
*$3,000.00 off any upgrade package
when you buy/build a Sagebrook home*

☐ **Sam Rafoss**
27% discount

☐ **The Silk Road Spice Merchant**
15% discount

☐ **Skintelligence Ltd.**
10% discount

☐ **The Social Page**
10% discount

☐ **Sol Swimwear**
*20% Off Sol Swimwear
boutique purchases*

☐ **Stephanie Pollock Media Inc.**
20% off an Activator Session

☐ **SweptAway Green Cleaning**
20% discount on first clean

☐ **ThairAPY Serenity and Beauty Services**
25% discount

☐ **Twisted Goods**
20% discount

☐ **Urban Venus Nail Bar**
*free Urban Venus nail polish when
you purchase a spa pedicure*

☐ **Vision 2000 Travel**
save $50 on your next vacation or cruise

☐ **Visual Hues Photography Inc.**
15% savings on print and canvas

☐ **The Willows Spa**
20% discount

☐ **Wine, Women and a Paintbrush**
20% discount

☐ **Work in Order**
free one-hour consultation

☐ **Your Friendly Bookkeeper**
10% off a full years' bookkeeping service

☐ **Your Space By Design**
15% discount

Use code CRAVE for online discount when applicable

Details of discounts may vary from business to business, so please call first.
The CRAVE company shall not be held responsible for variations on discounts at
individual businesses. This page may not be photocopied or otherwise duplicated.